SWINGER STYLE

JAYNE RYLON

OTHER BOOKS BY JAYNE RYLON

DIVEMASTERS
Going Down
Going Deep
Going Hard

MEN IN BLUE
Night is Darkest
Razor's Edge
Mistress's Master
Spread Your Wings
Wounded Hearts
Bound For You

POWERTOOLS
Kate's Crew
Morgan's Surprise
Kayla's Gift
Devon's Pair
Nailed to the Wall
Hammer it Home

HOTRODS

King Cobra
Mustang Sally
Super Nova
Rebel on the Run
Swinger Style
Barracuda's Heart
Touch of Amber
Long Time Coming

COMPASS BROTHERS

Northern Exposure
Southern Comfort
Eastern Ambitions
Western Ties

COMPASS GIRLS

Winter's Thaw
Hope Springs
Summer Fling
Falling Softly

PLAY DOCTOR

Dream Machine
Healing Touch

<u>STANDALONES</u>
4-Ever Theirs
Nice & Naughty
Where There's Smoke
Report For Booty

<u>RACING FOR LOVE</u>
Driven
Shifting Gears

<u>RED LIGHT</u>
Through My Window
Star
Can't Buy Love
Free For All

<u>PARANORMALS</u>
Picture Perfect
Reborn
<u>PICK YOUR PLEASURES</u>
Pick Your Pleasure
Pick Your Pleasure 2

DEDICATION

For all the readers who have been super fans long enough to become friends. Your support of my work is eternally appreciated. Phuong Phan, Liz Berry, Shirley Long, Cherie Clark, Tracey Reid, Fedora Chen, Barbara Kidd, Kitty Kelly, Casey Lu Matte, Gigi Staub, Dawn Vaeoso, Shari David, Charity Hendry, Terri & Billy Doughty, Nicole Harvey, Stacia Smith, Jen Salmi, Eileen Roth, Meghan Kinch, Linda Johnson, Zina Lynch, Susan Romito, all the Bitches and so, so, so many more. Thank you!

CHAPTER ONE

Sabra Harp slapped her palms onto the weathered door of the Bad News Bar and shoved it open, trundling through in time to avoid getting smacked in the face by its recoil. She didn't give a shit that her blouse had come untucked or that her mascara had left smudges on her cheeks when she'd dashed tears from them earlier.

On other days, the pub's name had seemed ironic. Today, fitting.

Weaving through the after-work crowd, she ignored the appreciative stares of the men pressing around her. All she needed right then was a good, stiff...*drink.*

She climbed onto the only empty stool at the bar and discouraged chitchat with the too-chipper plastic woman beside her by shooting off a death-ray glare. Then she turned to the bartender. "Hey, Ward, get me a rum and Coke, please."

"That's a far cry from your usual, nursing a few sips of our crappy house white when you show up at happy hour with those newsroom fellows. You sure?" He wrung his towel as he studied her. Dropping her gaze, she hoped he didn't notice how puffy and bloodshot her eyes were.

"Yeah. It's been that kind of day, you know? In fact, make it a double. With top shelf, strong shit." She planted her elbows on the bar and put her head in her hands without waiting for his response.

"I'll be right back with that, doll." He touched her wrist softly, then vanished.

"Having a rough one, huh?" The saccharine, singsongy question could only have come from the barfly next door. Damn it.

"Yes," Sabra spat through gritted teeth. Instead of taking the hint, the woman scooted her stool closer. *Great.*

"I know what that's like." The woman chuckled and patted Sabra on the shoulder. Unlike Ward's glancing contact, the connection had her skin crawling. Maybe it'd been a mistake to come here when she needed to stew. She'd finish her drink, then head home—alone—to mope in private.

"Yeah? What'd you do, break a nail?" Sabra knew she was being a bitch, but her filter had disintegrated earlier, along with her career as Middletown's anchorwoman. Telling one's boss to fuck off wasn't exactly a recommended path to promotions.

"Nah, boy trouble. What else?" Her neighbor's shrill laugh had several men turning their heads. Did fake dramatics like that really lure in guys? Admittedly drunk and rowdy, some of the interested dudes seemed like they should know better. "My name's Bambi, by the way."

Sabra realized her life could actually be worse. She could be called *Bambi*.

"Wow. Were your parents Disney fans or something?" She promised herself she'd quit the snark. Soon. It only steeped her in negativity instead of cheering her up. Probably she should have indulged in a double session of yoga and meditation instead of liquor. That might have cleared her mind instead of poisoning her chakras. Too late now.

There'd be plenty of time to practice the advanced jivamukti poses she'd nearly mastered now that she had joined the ranks of the jobless. Endless hours would abound after she finished out her two-week notice. They would allow her to concentrate on her core values and figure out what path to take from here. Kicking off the rest of her life with a hangover seemed like a minor indulgence.

"Huh?" Bambi's over-processed, super-styled platinum blonde hair didn't budge when she canted her head and squinted her eyes. "Actually, I picked it myself. My real name is Theresa. Do I look like a *Theresa* to you?"

"Hell no, baby," a smashed man answered for Sabra.

She prayed the two would hit it off and sneak into the woods out back for a quickie. No such luck.

"Thanks, sugar." Bambi winked, then returned her attention to Sabra.

When Ward delivered her drink with a slight shake of his head, she didn't hesitate in downing a slug and then another. A welcome burn spread through her chest, masking the chill inside her, at least for a moment or two. Until she guzzled a few more swallows.

"So, like I was saying, I've had a bad run here lately." Bambi flounced and swiveled so that she faced Sabra fully. Her cleavage stayed remarkably steady since her unnaturally large boobs didn't wobble even a bit. Kind of fascinated, Sabra tried not to stare, draining more of her rum and Coke instead.

"First, a guy I really liked clocked me, so I had to ditch him. Then I decided to go for some pure fun with a couple of mechanics. But they ended up wanting to screw each other more than me. And when I tried a boring accountant instead, the guy dumped me just because I gave his friend a hummer in the bathroom when we were smashed one night. I mean, it *was* the guy's birthday. Go figure."

"Rewind. Did you say *mechanics*?" An entire lifetime of ferreting out leads kicked in like second nature. Then again, Sabra had been kind of obsessed with a grease monkey herself lately. Too bad he couldn't stand her since she'd broken a promise to him.

"Oh, yeah." Bambi grinned, then leaned in closer to continue in a conspiratorial whisper-shout. "Mechanics*sssssssss*. There were two of them. Hot. One is this bald Latino guy, and the other is a real all-American kind of stud. Handsome and dangerous enough to get my motor running. I blew that guy once, out back, and hoped he'd return the favor by making me crazy along with his friends. I think there are six or seven of the guys who work in their shop. Well, anyway, a couple of them came in here, looking…sorta like you do tonight. So I tried to cheer them up. They banged me on some old car they were fixing. It should have been smoking. Except it kind of sucked. They weren't that into me. Can you believe that? I think they wanted each other more than me. Total disappointment."

Bambi rolled her eyes, as if such a thing was impossible.

Unfortunately, Sabra could picture it really well. Two guys she'd met recently blazed to the front of her mind. Eli London and Alanso Diaz. They fit Bambi's description like the designer wiggle dress Sabra had been eying as a reward for her next promotion, which hugged her curves and gave her flare worthy of a pin-up.

She drained her glass as she imagined the guys hooking up with each other and one of the ladies she'd seen in their company at the park that fateful day.

Don't ask. Don't ask. Don't ask.

Sabra couldn't help but torture herself. "Are you talking about the Hot Rods?"

"Holy cow!" Bambi's eyes grew wide as she shrieked, "Have you—"

"No. No, no and *no* again." Almost tipping over on her stool, Sabra waved off the thwarted question, frantically trying to get her new frenemy to lower her voice about a hundred decibels. "I know of them, but they hate my guts."

"Mine too, I think." Bambi frowned into her lite beer. "I was kind of a bitch to them. But we'd all been drinking and I was really horny."

"I could help you out with that." A guy invaded Bambi's personal space, circling like a vulture. He must have overheard enough of their conversation to sense opportunity. *Uh-oh.*

The room spun when Sabra jerked her head in the encroacher's direction quick enough to spot lust and overconfidence in the guy's stare.

"Back off, buddy." Ward collected Sabra's empty glass and reached to steady her. He glanced up as if watching someone else approach, except this time he nodded slightly instead of baring his teeth.

None of it mattered to Sabra. She couldn't believe her nose for news still functioned. So she tried to dig up more of the scoop.

"Bambi, you mean Eli and Alanso, right?" She reached toward the other woman. "What about Holden? The one they call Swinger. With the killer smile and the super-tight ass. Was he involved?"

"If there's something you want to know about me or my friends, why don't you come straight to the source?" The gruff question from directly behind her sounded more like an accusation than an expression of curiosity. "Or are you writing gossip columns instead of reporting the news these days?"

"Holden!" Of all the Hot Rods to stroll into this bar, he had to be the one to show up. Of course he did. Actually, while Sabra actively avoided Holden's glare, she thought she spotted Carver and Roman hovering around a high-top table near the pool table in the shady corner. How had she missed them when she'd stormed in?

This was officially the worst day of her life.

"Gotta go." Sabra wasn't proud. She made a run for it. Except her scramble off the stool nearly bowled over the nearest six losers, who crowded her spot at the bar as if eavesdropping on her and Bambi. Exactly how loud had they been?

Shit.

Holden's strong arm braced her until she gained her footing. Then he yanked away as if contaminated by her filth. His sneer told her exactly what he thought of the reporter who'd landed his friends in danger. The knife in her chest stabbed again and again.

The wounds were too raw to discuss. She had to get out before she bled to death.

Sabra dashed for the exit, doing her best to make a beeline for freedom. Escaping Holden's light brown, accusing stare. Certainly, she'd only pissed him off more with her prying. But damn, she couldn't deny that hearing Bambi's story, and wondering what it would be like to be the center of that much attention, had distracted her from her epic woes.

If only for a fleeting moment.

Fresh air filled her lungs as she gulped in the evening air. With her hands on her knees, she tried to make the world come into focus again. Hell, she'd drunk more in the past five minutes than she had in all the visits she'd made to Bad News in the couple years before that, and she'd always been a cheap date.

"Are you going to puke?" Instead of turning away, Holden surprised her by easing her toward the grass at the edge of the sidewalk, rubbing her lower back with gentle circles that did far more treacherous things to her insides than a few ounces of hundred-proof alcohol. When he gathered her hair in his fist and wrapped an arm around her middle as he held her from behind, her spine arched instinctively.

"No. I'm fine." *Liar*. She stood upright and tottered a few steps away, breaking his hold. "What'd you come out here for? To yell at me some more?"

Okay, so he hadn't actually screamed at her. Still, the tone of the email he'd shot off to her last week, bitching her out for exposing his friends to the bad guys hunting them, stuck in her mind. Those harsh accusations, and her resulting guilt, had driven her to clash with management and, ultimately, quit the job she adored. The one that had been her whole world. A responsibility she hadn't taken seriously enough.

"Not exactly." He didn't seem quite so sure. "I'm still pissed. And I don't appreciate people digging around in my family's personal shit. But you looked like you could use some help. Do you need a lift?"

"Nope." She marched toward her car, twisting her ankle in the process.

"Hey. Easy." He steadied her by braceleting her waist with his work-roughened fingers and edging closer once more. The contact burned through her wrinkled clothes and she flinched, wrenching from his grip. "I thought you'd just showed up. Were you in the bathroom or something before that? How the hell much did you chug?"

"Just one stupid drink." She told the truth through semi-numb lips, making the protest weak and fuzzy, like her mind. Alcohol and grief magnified her shock at everything she'd lost today. And how painful it would be to return to the newsroom each night for the next fourteen broadcasts, knowing her tenure was short-lived. The brutal argument she'd had with her boss, Mr. Grills, would only amplify the discomfort. He was known for being a vindictive son of a bitch.

After escaping Holden, she'd wait out her buzz in her locked car. Maybe take a nap or something before heading home. Slamming her drink on an empty stomach had probably been a mistake. She'd made plenty lately. What was one more?

"Well, I don't care, lightweight. Give me your keys. You're not driving like this. Are you fucking crazy? Kill yourself if you want, but *other* people out there are innocent. They don't deserve your reckless endangerment." Holden snatched her purse from her fingers with hardly any effort. When he caught her stunned—and hurt—gaze, he grimaced. "That sounded harsh. I wasn't talking about the other stuff. With Kae and Bryce, I mean."

"Whatever." She shoved his chest and tried to wobble in as straight a line as possible toward the road. If she had to walk to get away from him, she'd do it. His judgment stung, even if he didn't know she'd done the right thing in the end.

"Hey, wait." He jogged a few steps to catch up with her, U-turning her with mild pressure on her shoulder. Maybe because she secretly wanted to stop. To have company. Funny, when she compared isolation to spending time with him, being alone didn't seem so attractive after all. If only he didn't despise her. "Sorry, let me drive you. I'm not such a douche that I'd let a woman—*you*...wander home drunk by yourself."

"Do me a favor, okay?" She couldn't take anything else today.

"Sure." He scrubbed his hand through his hair then over the beard stubble she wanted to rub against like her cat when it smooshed its face against the corner of the couch in a compulsive scent-marking display.

"Don't talk to me. I can't argue right now. Not with you or anyone else. Shut up and drive. Fast." Sabra knew she was weak where this guy was concerned. His disgust had prompted her resignation. Shameless, she licked her lips as she scanned him from head to toe. Unruly hair, a strong jaw and a mouth that was quick to curve into a crooked smile—complete with dimples—for the right person. Badass prep defined his style. A soft, worn hoodie covered a Henley. A navy-and-gray wide-striped scarf somehow only made him look sexier instead of dorky. Trim and fit, she bet he had more definition than it appeared beneath his clothes. Jeans tattered by work and genuine wear versus a fashion factory hugged his perfect ass and framed his package just right. If he lingered, she might make another request of him. One she would regret in the morning. Like so many other things that had happened in the past twenty-four hours.

"Can do." He didn't ask for permission. Instead, he simply plucked her from the ground and swung her into his surprisingly strong arms. Within seconds, he'd used her fob to unlock her car, whisked her toward the vehicle that lit up in response, then deposited her gently on the passenger seat before rounding the hood to join her.

"Lincoln and Town, above the pizza shop," she instructed as if he were a cabbie instead of a hot-rodder. Sabra leaned her head on the window and tried not to catch glimpses of his capable handling as he quickly rearranged the mirrors then pulled onto the dark street, heading toward her apartment.

Why the hell did he have to choose now to reappear in her life?

She ignored the stinging in her eyes and the part of her that would love to unload on him. To confess what she'd done. Try to make amends. Or use him to erase the pain ripping her apart. Truth was, she didn't deserve him. It wouldn't be fair to either of them to cross those lines, tangling pleasure and pain, reminding them both of what had happened. Because of her.

When they pulled into the alley behind her apartment, she didn't know whether to be relieved or sad at how quickly they'd gotten there. It took her three tries to find her door handle. Holden appeared outside, opening it for her and hauling her from the vehicle before she had her shit together.

Pathetic. Why couldn't she do anything right around this man? And why did she want to prove to him that she wasn't as lame as he assumed she was?

He wrapped an arm around her waist and practically carried her up the exterior stairs. At the top, he used the only other key on her ring to unlock her apartment. When he attempted to usher her inside, she stumbled over the threshold, ending up plastered full-length against him.

Heat flared through her core. Before she could think better of it, she'd coiled her arms around his neck. With that much contact, she had no hope of resisting the magnetism between them. Instead, she fused their mouths. He didn't shove her away.

Several heartbeats pounded through her as Holden returned the kiss with interest, making her toes curl. If the world hadn't already been off kilter, he'd have tilted it on its axis. His taste, the suave seduction of his mouth on hers and his palms cupping her ass all combined to fire her up.

He inched forward, then pivoted, trapping her against the door jamb. His hands pinned her wrists over her head, and his body held her still as he plundered her parted lips.

Sabra let him take, allowed him to use her and guide them both through blazing pleasure. Her nipples dug into the firm heat of his chest. His hard cock nudged her belly as they strained toward each other. She gave herself into his care and he rewarded her trust with rapture.

Until he yanked backward. She nearly fell on her ass without his support.

"Damn you." He banged his fist on the doorframe above her head, making her jump. "That isn't what I came here for."

"S-sorry." A flush stained her cheeks. How much mortification could one woman withstand in a day? Quitting before she could get fired for insubordination had sucked. Holden's rejection was twice as bad. "Really. I screwed up. Everything."

Before he could reach out for her or bash her again—his disgust wounding her much more than fists ever could—she tucked inside and closed the door, locking him out of her home.

And her life.

Even then she couldn't help but peek at him, knowing it would be the last time she saw the man of her dreams. From behind the corner of a curtain, she watched him struggle with his too-tight jeans until he yanked his phone from his back pocket then swiped his thumb across its screen. After a brief pause, he said, "Pick me up at Tortelli's."

Holden pinched the bridge of his nose as he started slowly down her staircase.

"No. I'm *not* staying the night. I don't care how quick that was. If you get here in the next fifteen minutes, I'll buy you a fucking pizza. No. I don't need time for that either. Hurry up, Meep. I just want to go home. And not a word of this gets spilled to the rest of the guys or I'll tell them about the time you blacked out and pissed yourself, got it?"

Sabra stumbled away from the window as his voice faded when he picked up steam, jogging down the rest of the stairs. He hated her so much that he didn't want his friends to know he'd done her a simple favor?

She supposed she understood. Without the energy to find her bedroom or get undressed, she collapsed onto her sofa, hugged a pillow to her chest and buried her face in the cushions as she sobbed.

How would she survive the next two weeks until she went off the air permanently?

What would she do after that?

Part of her life had died today. Grieving for that, and a guy she'd never had to lose, took a lot of tears. Even after she'd cried herself dry, sleep refused to come as she racked her brain in an attempt to spawn possibilities for her future that didn't involve moving back home or selling organs. Distressed, Sir Clawdius Fuzzington meowed before head-butting her hip. He kneaded the tense muscles in the small of her back until she relaxed enough to make a decent bed for his majesty. Curling into a ball of fluff, he snoozed. At least one of them did.

Sometime after the first light of dawn filtered through her bamboo blinds, an idea came to her. Either genius or insane—maybe both—it refused to be discarded like the million other schemes she'd concocted in the darkest parts of the night.

Could she find the courage to try that?

Probably not. Unless desperation drove her to it.

She had two weeks to come up with a better idea. Anything else. But she didn't.

CHAPTER TWO

Sabra inhaled until her lungs threatened to either pop or shatter her rib cage. She released her breath in a controlled hiss her yoga instructor would have approved with a wise nod. Unfortunately, the exercise was an epic fail when it came to manufacturing some much-needed Zen.

Her car keys jingled in time to the trembling of her fingers as she marched toward the open bay doors of Hot Rods, the local restomod operation and service station. Home of the man who'd haunted her fantasies. Double-time since he'd proved their chemistry wasn't one-sided by giving her the best kiss of her life. A warm welcome was more than she had a right to expect. Beyond that, her intent to ask the eight mechanics who worked there for a favor pretty much guaranteed she should be checked into the loony bin. Pronto.

They had every reason to despise her. Some of them more than others after their run-in three weeks ago. Hell, she kind of loathed herself. Trust her to ruin an ideal wedding proposal she'd stumbled across in the park by turning it into a feature. The allure of leading the nightly news with a happy headline for once had reeled her in. How could she have predicted the fiasco that had followed her report on the heartwarming story?

Well, Holden *had* warned her not to include the hulking, dark-haired guy, Bryce, and his gorgeous girlfriend, Kaelyn, in her segment. Though she'd passed along the editing instructions, she hadn't done enough to ensure they were followed. Her failure had cost them all.

And broken her heart, in a bunch of different ways.

The group of mechanics who'd collaborated to celebrate their friends' milestone moment had touched her. A shit ton of other people too, if you believed the stratospheric ratings for that edition of the five o'clock broadcast. The video clip had gone viral as millions sighed over the ultra-romantic production. It made her realize what she might have sacrificed for her career—meaningful interpersonal relationships. Beyond the ones she had with her makeup artist and wardrobe department or the other newshounds who chased breaking stories, always cutthroat, trying to scoop each other.

The Hot Rods' pure friendships—and more—had changed her. Or at least they'd been the catalyst, initiating a reaction in her that had corroded some of her commitment to her life goals and the things she'd considered most important.

So when the gang of mechanics had been threatened by that exposure, indirectly because of Sabra, she'd done what she could to control the damage. People like them deserved to be happy.

Despite the implosion of her own dreams.

It hadn't been easy to land the anchorwoman position, even in a moderate city like Middletown. A few more years and she'd have clawed up to a more prestigious regional network on her way to a national program. Well, that had been the plan before everything went to hell.

Getting any of the major players in the industry to take her seriously without references would be as challenging as the expert-level asana—Two Leg Pose of the Sage Koundinya—she'd attempted at the end of every workout for the past six months. Each time falling flat on her face. Failure didn't stop her from trying.

Securing a good word from her ex-boss, Redford Grills... Well, *that* would be impossible since she'd told him to fuck off after refusing to play by his rules. At first, the reality of her greater sacrifice had hurt more than the dozens of sprained wrists she'd inflicted on herself before crashing into her yoga mat.

Then humiliating herself by throwing herself at Holden had plunged her straight to the bottom of her personal barrel. With nothing left to lose, she'd cooked up an alternative based on rumblings from the station.

It might be the psycho-genius kind of brilliant. A teensy step short of stalkerish. Nevertheless, she'd run out of options, and despite the billions of times she'd second-guessed herself since then, the light bulb hovering over her head refused to extinguish.

Thinking about it—obsessively, maybe—had been a hell of a lot easier than taking action, though. Her footsteps slowed as she neared, concentrating on how she planned to evolve instead of being buried alive by her mountain of regrets.

Where was the whir and grind of power tools? No shouting, banging or loud music filtered through the garage that loomed in front of her.

Journalistic instincts kicked in.

Sabra edged closer, peeking into the cavernous interior from behind the cinderblock strip that separated two of the drive-through doorways. As her eyes adjusted, she detected the ripped forms of the Hot Rods, who hovered around their ladies, less than twenty feet from her outpost.

What were they doing in there?

Were the rumors she'd heard about their kinkiness true? As a journalist—one who believed in integrity and doing her job right— she found it tough to trust any single source. Especially when her tip had come from a bitter, overdone barfly. *Especially* especially one who called herself Bambi. After the night at Bad News, Sabra had done some research, poking around inconspicuously.

It was second nature to tease secrets from strangers.

Though she'd hardly had to make an effort when she'd uncovered a couple women, like Bambi, who couldn't wait to blab about their sexual gymnastics. Sabra didn't object to the women's uninhibited exploration. Their lack of discretion... Well, that sucked for their playmates, whom they'd been willing—no, *eager*—to name.

Besides, something about Bambi's account had rung true, even after Sabra's buzz had cleared. Maybe it had been Bambi's disappointment that the guys seemed into each other. Sabra had picked up on that vibe herself when she'd tagged along to the engagement party in the park. Smoldering glances tossed between any variety of the mechanics had threatened to scorch the conservative navy suit her station had required. Only difference was that sizzle had turned her on instead of pissing her off.

If Bambi had actually been lucky enough to indulge both the garage owner and his spicy Latino friend simultaneously, she had every right to brag. They were enough to overheat Sabra's motor solo, never mind together. The only thing hotter would have been if Holden had joined in the fray, using his dipstick to check her oil. Repeatedly.

Then again, it seemed more probable that Bambi had switcherooed herself and Mustang Sally, the garage's only female mechanic and paint job specialist, in that fantasy matchup. There were people in Middletown who swore Sally—nicknamed for her pink convertible, and maybe her predisposition to riding—had recently claimed the pair for herself in an unconventional wedding ceremony, right out back of this very garage, which the gang lived above.

Sabra wished she'd stumbled across *that* while nosing around about the Hot Rods, which she admitted to herself she'd done since they'd met. Both in the interests of her professional pursuits and to appease her personal curiosity.

Damn her reliable Acura for never needing service.

Watching the Hot Rods now, she didn't find it farfetched that they might enjoy getting it on together. They stood close, muscled biceps and broad chests forming a wall of flesh as they beamed at Kaelyn and her man, Bryce. Casual touches, intimate stares and a support system she could practically see propped each other up, protecting those at the center.

She swallowed hard.

Certainly they wouldn't be fooling around in broad daylight. Would they?

She leaned forward, pressing her thighs together, secretly hoping they might.

Instead, she saw Bryce rise from where he'd been crouched behind his might-as-well-be-a-super-model girlfriend. The husk in his voice made Sabra's knees weak when he growled, "I love it, Kaelyn."

Holden—the hottest guy in the pack of sexy beasts, as far as Sabra was concerned—seemed to be tending to a bandage on the ass of his best friend's woman. Compact, he didn't fool her—beneath those coveralls, he sported the contoured musculature she loved best on a man. Lean and defined. Not too big for her petite frame. He'd fit her body as if custom-made when they'd locked lips on her landing.

His familiar touch on Kaeyln's curves inspired a pinch of jealousy along with a bunch of wicked daydreams where Sabra substituted herself into the middle of a grease monkey sandwich. Yet the glint in his eyes, which complemented his quicksilver grin as he flickered from brooding to mischievous, tugged at more lethal parts of her anatomy.

Ink flashed through his fingers. A tattoo. Kaelyn had permanently painted a brand onto her skin. The Hot Rods logo. *Well, that's one way to declare your forever intent.*

Sabra had learned a lot about the ex-socialite since accidentally revealing her whereabouts to the woman's shady father, who'd been hunting her. Though Kaelyn DuChamp had only stumbled across the mechanics—including her long-lost bestie, Bryce—recently, her lust and adoration had been obvious the first time Sabra had run into the pair on that ill-fated afternoon in the park.

It wasn't hard to understand why a woman would be drawn to this collection of guys, as powerful, built and enticing as the muscle cars they were nicknamed after. Bryce continued to murmur to Kaelyn as he cupped her face and then grabbed her other cheeks, below the belt, deliberately though gently squeezing the promise she'd indelibly etched there.

When the woman sniffled and gazed at the circle of friends around her, the electricity of their bond sparked so bright, Sabra almost dove for the protection of the welding mask lying on the station in front of her. Something about how they shuffled closer to each other, and the intensity of their stares, boosted the temperature in the garage by at least ten degrees.

Or maybe that was her internal thermostat going haywire.

Sabra fanned her face and considered heading back to her car. Driving around the block a few dozen times with the air-conditioning set on arctic might cool her off enough that she could try to approach them again without short-circuiting her brain. Interrupting personal moments seemed to be a particular talent of hers when it came to this motley group.

They intrigued her. She couldn't be the only one who'd be mesmerized by their intricate friendship. With that thought, she bucked up. It was now or never.

And she didn't have a lot of options left.

"Excuse me." Sabra cleared her throat, unsure if they could hear her desperate croak. "Is anyone around?"

Didn't it figure that Holden spun forward first? Closest, he charged toward her, both blocking her view of the scene behind him and crushing her hopes with his raised hackles, accompanied by a snarl worthy of a lion protecting its pride.

Sabra propped her hands on her hips, relying on bravado to help her survive his hostility. Or maybe he did everything with such intensity. Undiluted, his passion had rocked her through one not-so-simple kiss.

"What do *you* want?" he snapped. Still, she caught a flash of something smoldering in his gaze as he clasped his hands in front of him. Was he trying to hide the impressive bulge in his jeans? If so, he failed miserably. Inquiring minds wanted to know... Did she have something to do with it, or had Kaelyn and Bryce's romance inspired his wood?

She shook her head to clear it, concentrating on the reason she'd sought him out.

"First, I came to apologize." Sabra gazed into his eyes, studying gold flecks buried in his almond irises. She wanted him to understand how genuine her statement was.

Regardless of his response, she had to get something off her chest before she kicked the hornet's nest again. "I know it doesn't matter, but I told my producer they couldn't use the clips of Kaelyn and Bryce and to cut them from the program. At the last second, they decided the emotional impact of your friends celebrating was too good for the editing room floor. I didn't know they were going to put it in the piece it until it was too late."

"Yeah, but you handed over the recording to them. With every bit included." He invaded her space, blasting her with the heat of his fury. Not to mention his potent sensuality.

"I know, and for that I'm sorry. I trusted them. I shouldn't have." She glanced away. It was that or give in to the urge to trace his stubbled jaw with her index finger. Or her tongue. Again. "Anyway, I don't work there anymore."

"Yeah, right. I saw you on the news last night." He grimaced, as if he hadn't meant to admit it.

"You did?" A smile tugged at the corners of her lips no matter how hard she tried to keep her poker face in place for the negotiations that hopefully lay ahead.

"Oh yeah," Roman piped up. "Swinger here is a regular broadcast addict lately.

Didn't know you were that concerned with current events, buddy."

Swinger put one hand behind his back. If Sabra had to guess, he flipped his garagemate the bird. A couple chuckles broke out. Maybe not all of the Hot Rods wanted to grind her into dust.

Only the one guy she wished didn't believe in holding a grudge seemed offended by her presence.

"Well, anyway... I gave them two weeks' notice, then quit." Sabra sighed. "I thought I should come by in person and tell you how sorry I am that my bad choice put you in danger. I didn't realize the full repercussions until I got your—uh—blunt email. I'm honestly sorry."

Kaelyn, redressed, edged up beside Holden and reached out, enfolding Sabra in a spontaneous, and very unexpected, hug. A rush of emotions flooded her system. Horrified, she tamped down the stinging in her eyes.

"It's okay. Don't worry about it anymore. Everything worked out. I've made my own share of bad decisions, especially when it comes to believing people who don't deserve your trust." Kaelyn offered her a grim smile along with a shake of her platinum mane.

"No one here is innocent." Eli strode forward, every bit the King Cobra the Hot Rods had referred to him as during her interviews the day of the proposal. "I've hurt people I care about. Deeply. It's how you make it up to them, and how you go forward that counts."

"Thank you." Sabra clung to the lifeline he tossed her. She attempted to blink away moisture before it spilled, her gaze averted so she didn't have to see the disagreement in Holden's eyes.

He huffed from beside them, drawing her attention despite her best intentions. The corners of his mouth pinched in a frown. "And what else?"

She concentrated on not biting her lip. It was true. She could have emailed him or called the garage anytime to ask for forgiveness. His car-shaped business card— the one he'd slipped her in the park—had tattered edges from her endless fingering these past few weeks. Not all of the hours she'd spent flipping it between her knuckles had been spent thinking about her professional request.

Plus, any investigator worth her salt could look up the Hot Rods website, including his contact info, courtesy of Google. She'd spent more time than she cared to admit surfing the

About section of their page, memorizing each guy, his favorite car and nickname. A matching fangirl tattoo on her own ass might be the next step if she wasn't careful.

"Swinger." Carver issued a low warning and touched Holden's elbow.

She figured she wouldn't get a better opening.

"I have a business proposition for you—" She paused and whipped her stare to Holden when he growled.

He mumbled, "I knew it."

Then she stood straighter, put her shoulders back and blurted, "I've done some research. Since I'm currently unemployed, I have an idea. Something I think could be big. And it involves you guys."

"We're not interested," Holden barked.

"Let the woman speak, Swinger." Eli's command silenced Holden, giving Sabra the chance she needed. It surprised her when the rest of the Hot Rods paid close attention.

Carver slapped Holden on the back. "Come on, I bet this is going to be good."

She hoped he still thought so after she dropped her bomb. Nothing for it now other than to spit it out. "I want to produce a reality show, with you guys as the stars."

Kaige laughed so hard he choked. Blond dreads swirled around his handsome face as he broke into a coughing fit. His fiancée, Nola, slapped him on the back when she peered at Sabra. "You're not joking, are you?"

"Nope." Though Super Nova's response probably told her everything she needed to know.

"What? People don't give a shit about our daily lives." Alanso spoke without flinging daggers at her with his tone, though he rubbed his bald head while thinking. Beside him, Sally nodded in agreement.

Very unlike the animosity radiating from Holden in waves. He hated her idea as much as he disliked her. And he made no point of hiding it.

"We're simple people. Boring, really," Bryce added.

Someone—maybe Roman—snorted from behind the big man. Usually serious, his outburst drew smiles from several of his garagemates.

"You know what I mean, asshole." Bryce rolled his eyes.

Then nearly all of the guys focused on her at once, as if thinking in tune with each other. She wouldn't be surprised if they did.

"What?" She put her hands up, palms out, then took a step back as the unrelenting force of their combined attention hit her.

"What *exactly* would this show be about?" Eli asked.

"Oh, you know, something where we focus on your customers and the cars they bring to you to fix up. Maybe we'd talk about the history of each automobile, the make and model, what's significant about that piece. Hopefully there would be some interesting back story on where your customer got the beat-up car from. Then we could show you working your magic and the finished product. With some shop banter and personality pieces added to reel in the reality show junkies. Nothing too overdramatized, though. I can't stand that crap."

Holden let out a long breath. He stepped toward her, narrowing her world to him and only him. Difficult to do in the presence of so much testosterone.

"A girl like you doesn't just come in here and throw out a suggestion like this. How much *research* have you done on Hot Rods?" He crowded her, his steadying fingers warm on her forearm when she jerked in response. "What do you know? You were grilling Bambi about us at the Bad News Bar. And I don't think you give a shit about how good we are as mechanics, either."

"I *still* can't believe you put your dick in her," Roman mumbled as he shook his head and punched Alanso in the arm. A muscle ticked in Sally's jaw. Okay, this wasn't going in a productive direction.

No sense in fucking around. Or lying.

"Are you wondering if I've unearthed rumors about your sex lives?" Sabra shivered when she challenged him.

"Yeah, I guess that's what I'm asking." Holden stared down at her with an impassive mask she didn't buy for a second. If he waited for her to kick him in the nuts or belittle him for his sexual preferences, he'd be standing there a hell of a long time.

"I've heard stuff." She shrugged. "But I don't see where it has anything to do with me. Or the show."

"I bet it could be very relevant to you, honey." Carver winked at her, then glanced toward Holden, who'd started gnashing his teeth.

Sabra tried not to react to his goading, refusing to let their antics distract her. Her shock and disbelief must have shown through regardless.

"She's obviously a prude." Holden sneered. In that moment, she kind of hated him.

"Screw you. You're the one who shut down our kiss as if you were afraid I had cooties. Don't you dare pretend otherwise or put words in my mouth." She crossed her arms.

"It ain't words he wants to feed you," Roman muttered, though loud enough for her to barely make out his smartassery.

Meanwhile, several of the other people witnessing their meltdown flicked gazes at each other.

Oops. Maybe she shouldn't have mentioned making out with Holden. Too damn bad.

Her sudden flush had nothing to do with outrage, and everything to do with desire, but they didn't have to know that. Especially not if she wanted them to take her—and her project—seriously. "Look, what you do behind these rolling doors is your business. I'm not some judgmental conservative. And I'm not looking to exploit your sexuality either. So keep your thoughts about mine to your damn selves."

"Ouch." Eli grinned as he thumped Holden on the back. "She's kind of got a point there. Stop being an asshole."

Nola squeezed through the crowd to join Sabra and Kaelyn. Kind and welcome, her smile illuminated her face. "Thank you for the offer. I know it couldn't have been easy for you to come here today. I appreciate a woman who grabs opportunity by the balls. A good idea is a good idea. And I think you could be on to something here."

"Are you nuts?" Holden's slack jaw might have been amusing under other circumstances.

"Maybe for hanging around the lot of you." Nola ruffled his hair, disarming his fuming before angling toward Eli, the garage owner. "Think about it. This could be excellent advertising for the shop. I can't buy this kind of exposure for us, Cobra."

"Exactly." Sabra latched on to the lifeline. She waved to the public space around them and shrugged. "I'm talking about a documentary of industry-related, doors-open, stuff. Show off your best work to millions."

If our local station will take on the show and if the national network selects it as their mid-season replacement after I produce and pitch a kickass pilot. It was a lot of ifs.

"Shit." Eli scrubbed his hands through his hair. Both Alanso and Sally licked their lips when he did.

A shiver ran through Sabra, but she chanted *focus, focus, focus* internally until she got her mind on professional matters. This impartial bullshit might be harder to fake than she'd imagined.

"I can see your point, Nola." Cobra rested a hand on Holden's shoulder and squeezed.

"And Swinger's concerns. Not to mention that we bought Kaelyn's and Bryce's freedoms from their crazy families by promising to keep them out of the limelight. Tricky to get around that. I think this calls for a garage meeting. With Tom and Ms. Brown too. We shouldn't do anything stupid. Or hasty."

"I couldn't agree more." Holden crossed his arms then relaxed, as did Nola.

Who would win?

"Can you give us a day or two to talk this over?" Eli asked.

"Sure." Sabra hadn't dared to hope for that much. She winced as she realized how unprepared she'd been for success. Their timeline was tight if she was going to hit the deadline for the replacement search. "Let me give you my cell number since the email address Holden blasted me at is junk these days, now that I'm done at the station. Do you have something to write on?"

She fished for a pen in her purse.

"Here." Holden held out his hand. "If I'm lucky, it'll smudge next time I take a piss."

Terrific. Now she was thinking about him strangling his junk while she cupped his fingers in her palm. Thankfully, she didn't have to deliver a witty comeback when someone smacked him upside the head for her.

If she caressed his dinged knuckles a bit more than necessary, too fucking bad. It was his fault for being so sexy, even sullen.

The sharp intake of his breath was only audible since she was so close to him. She might have thought she scratched him with the sharp tip of her pen, if she hadn't gotten zapped by the corresponding jolt of electricity their connection generated. It had her hair standing on end as she finished marking her info on his calloused palm.

"Are you going to tell her we'll be *in touch*, Swinger?" Carver broke the tension as Holden and Sabra stepped away from each other, neither meeting the other's gaze.

"What he said." Holden's gruff reply proved he hadn't been unaffected by their contact.

"I appreciate you considering the show." Sabra held her head high and scanned the gang of mechanics. She smiled at Kaelyn and Bryce, who nodded in return. "Have a good day."

Without surrendering to the urge to peek at Holden again, she pivoted on her kitten heels and headed for her car. The Hot Rods' stares heated her straight spine as she crossed the lot.

"Hey, Sabra." Holden stopped her instantly with his shout.

Holding her breath, she turned to face him as he jogged after her. Her head tipped as she asked, "Yes?"

"Thank you for doing the decent thing. About the footage of Bryce and Kae, I mean." His stare assessed her with something that touched her deeper than their attraction. Grudging respect. "I shouldn't have been such a dick and assumed it was your fault."

No matter what happened when she left, she'd have won that, at least.

It was something. Something big to her. Soon, it might be the only thing she had.

Unsure of how to respond, she swallowed hard, then nodded before climbing into her car. He didn't stop her again. But when she glanced in her rearview mirror, he was still standing there—boots planted on the pavement, legs spread, hands jammed in his torn pockets—watching her go, instead of rejoining the group of friends who waited for him inside.

With her future in their hands.

And the power to crush it.

CHAPTER THREE

"You kids have to quit this baloney already." Tom London's scowl couldn't hide his affection. "I mean, we *just* got rid of Senator Assmunch and his arch nemesis sidekick and you're already calling another garage meeting? What now? Did someone discover a lost twin? Have a deep, dark secret they have to reveal? Succumb to an early mid-life crisis? Unearth buried treasure beneath the junk heap? Well, that last one wouldn't be so terrible. I swear, we could practically have our own freaking TV show with all this drama lately."

"Funny you should say that." Eli patted his dad on the back, then stepped away before he divulged the reason behind their gathering.

Holden hated the tension in the room, between his friends and their quasi-parental-units—Eli's dad and Nola's mom.

"Let the kids talk." Ms. Brown snipped at Tom. No *Tommy*-this or *Tommy*-that from her today. No mushy stuff either. Holden wondered what his stand-in father had done to land himself in the doghouse. Whatever it was might account for his sudden crankypants act.

When the Hot Rods turned as one and stared at Holden, he groaned.

"What stunt did you pull, Swinger?" Tom crossed his arms and tapped his foot. "Try to prank someone who didn't laugh at your antics this time?"

"I didn't do jack shit. It's these morons who are trying to land us in a giant pile of steaming turds." He pointed at his garagemates, who littered the sectional sofa and the other furniture in their enormous living area.

"It's not a bad suggestion, Holden." Nola's soft rebuke made it harder to argue. He had no desire to fight with her. "Come on. Tell him what Sabra wants to do."

"Sabra?" Tom tilted his head. His eyes narrowed and he leaned in closer, like a dog on the hunt. "Sabra *Harp*? Your crush from the local news?"

"Yeah, her." The gruffness to Holden's tone had everything to do with the rapid rush of blood below his belt. No point in denying it. These people knew him too damn well. He shifted in his seat to cover his lap with his arms.

Why had she looked extra fine when she'd allowed them to glimpse a side of her he'd bet no one else saw? A hint of vulnerability. She'd practically begged them to save her career.

It wasn't that he didn't want to help her. More like he wanted to give in too much. Too fast. Too easy. And that freaked him out. Just like it had the night he'd escorted her home then claimed his bonus.

Damn, that had been the single best kiss he'd ever stolen from a woman. Or maybe she'd been the one to launch a sneak attack. Either way, he'd lost his mind for a moment, thinking only of memorizing her taste and fusing their bodies. Breaking away had been necessary to avoid tumbling into the paradise she offered, with no way out. Because while he usually preferred a sweaty bout of no-strings sex, something he didn't want to acknowledge told him that might not be possible when it came to Sabra Harp. Weeks later, he couldn't decide if he'd been wise or plain old stupid to reject her advance.

His dick voted emphatically for checking the box next to "moronic".

Impulsive, Holden had spent a good deal of his life rushing into things he should know better than to do. As he matured, he was working on taking things more seriously and assessing the consequences of his actions before succumbing to kneejerk reactions. Even he could see that rescuing this damsel in distress had the potential to unleash a world of trouble. The thrill of being her hero would come at the price of putting his friends at risk, exposing them and their special bond to millions of prying eyes. Again.

Especially because he was so damn attracted to her. He wouldn't be able to remain guarded. It just wasn't in his nature. Not with anyone, really, but definitely not around her. He was a sucker when it came to affection.

Adorable, Sabra was tougher than her pert features and petite frame suggested. He'd felt the strength in her arms when they'd hugged him to her. Her body hadn't been as pliant as he'd expected either. Instead of softness, he'd discovered toned muscle beneath his hands. The power in her had only riled him, not disappointed. That forcefulness wrapped in femininity drew him and gave him false hope that she might be able to handle the Hot Rods rowdy brand of loving.

Worse, something about her made it difficult to lump her in with the rest of the random women he'd like to fuck—in a simple carnal exchange. A good time was one thing, something he indulged in regularly. A commitment, loyalty, a connection that went beyond a very satisfying night in the sack—well, those things were reserved for the only people who'd ever proved themselves worthy. His Hot Rods.

Carver snapped Holden out of his wandering thoughts with a kick from his steel-toed boot. "Hurry up already. Tell him what your girlfriend wanted."

"She's not—"

"Don't let him rile you, Swinger." Tom shut them both up with a glare. "Stick to the facts. What did Sabra call about?"

"Huh?" Holden shook his head as he remembered the way her tight ass had looked in the sexy jeans that had hugged her perfect curves when she'd walked away. Petite yet fit. Hints of sinew had shown in her arms beneath her delicate blouse too. "She came in person."

"Must have been important, then," Ms. Brown murmured, inadvertently edging closer to Tom as she listened intently. "Nobody does things properly anymore. Face-to-face."

"It was. She came to apologize for letting Bryce and Kaelyn show up in her report." Holden grimaced as he remembered how frightened he'd been for his friends, knowing their fathers would easily track them down after they'd been broadcast to hundreds of thousands of living rooms. So probably he could admit that he'd overreacted, blasting Sabra when he didn't know how to fight the real danger threatening them. Could he owe her an apology too? *Fuck*.

"Decent of her." Tom smiled, confirming Holden's suspicions. "Everyone makes mistakes, Swinger. We ought to know that around here. So, did you ask her out after that?"

"No." He grimaced.

Why hadn't he? Any other time a woman revved him up like she had, he'd have sweet-talked her panties off in less time than it took to install a prefab bucket seat. With Sabra, he'd kept himself from doing exactly that. Even though his hand might be developing new calluses from the sheer number of jack-off sessions he'd held in her honor these past few weeks, he'd turned her down. None too gently either. Worse, he hadn't fixed that temporary insanity when she'd given him a golden opportunity.

Mustang Sally piped in. "She probably would have smacked him. I would have. You were so fucking rude to her. Asshole."

Holden winced. He had been kind of a shithead, but it was impossible to smother the reaction she caused to flare, burning him inside like the hellish indigestion he'd suffered after scarfing half a pizza with Carver the night he'd taken her home. He figured it served him right for denying them both. And since he hadn't vented his sexual tension through seduction, his pissy mood had been the only other option.

"So you think we should do it?" He glared at Sally. Of all of them, how could Mustang want to give Sabra the green light? It'd be obvious to anyone watching that Sally belonged to not one but two of the mechanics.

Eli and Alanso huddled closer to her, each laying a hand on one of her thighs. Damn straight. They'd have to watch her back and each other's. Not everyone in the world could claim to be as open-minded as their circle of friends.

"Do *what*?" Tom growled as he glanced between them.

"She wants to turn us into a circus act." Holden flung his hands out. "Show the world what freaks we are, one hour a week."

"That's not how I took it." Nola stood. "If that's what you think, maybe you're the one with the problem, Swinger. Are you ashamed of us? Of how we are?"

He jerked his head as if slapped. "Never."

"Back the hell up, kids. You lost me." Tom jerked his chin between them. Roman, who was already standing, obeyed the silent command, easing Nola onto Kaige's lap, returning her to her lover so they could gain some space to think properly. Nova surrounded his soon-to-be wife with his arms. Though he didn't feel the need to fight her battles, he was always there, ready to support her if necessary. Then Barracuda sat by Holden, letting him know it wasn't a case of him versus the rest of the gang.

Carver flanked him.

Being the center of a Meep-and-Roman sandwich calmed Holden, though it also proved his point. How many people would understand this complex bond when they hardly did?

And they lived it. Breathed it. Sweated it.

Hiding it from any careful observer would be impossible.

"What are you saying, Swinger?" Tom prodded him once more.

"Sabra spun some hype, trying to sell us on doing a TV show about the garage," Holden surrendered. He spread his knees, braced his forearms on his legs and hung his head. Going against everyone would be impossible. If they outvoted him, he'd be along for the ride. He could already feel it coming and knew he'd have a hell of a time keeping himself from breaking an axle given the potholes strewn in the road ahead.

"Oh! Really? I always wanted to be an actress. Do they have red carpets for television starlets?" Ms. Brown squeaked and clasped her hands in front of her, sighing. Another point for Team Sabra. *Shit.*

"Well, here's your chance, Mom. I'm sure we could sneak you into an episode or two." Nola smiled warmly at her mother. "Sabra's going to showcase the team's projects, and the mechanics themselves. It'll be great for business. Advertising like this is impossible to put a price on."

"But what about the impact to our lives? Nothing's free, Nola. What will this cost us?" Going down swinging, Holden made one-last ditch effort. "We'll have to watch everything we do, everything we say. The freedom to be ourselves will disappear. That's more important to me than success. We already have all we've dreamed of, don't we? Why be greedy?"

Roman put his hand on Holden's shoulder and squeezed. "I get why you're worried."

"You do?" He looked up at the hardened guy. Barracuda, private to the max, had only recently started exploring a bond deeper than friendship with Meep. Would having a camera in his face day in and day out screw with him too?

"Yeah. But—" Roman glanced at Carver, silently begging the guy to help him out.

"Don't act like you aren't as ambitious as the rest of us, Swinger." Meep picked up where his roommate trailed off. "We can keep our hands to ourselves during the day. It's not like we're mauling each other in the garage. We work hard. Let's show people what we're best at and take this operation to the next level. There were plenty of things in Kaige and Nola's roadmap for the shop that you were excited about. Doing the show could make everything happen quicker. We'll reach our goals sooner. Just think about that new double-head laser cutter you want for customizing leather upholstery. Maybe it's only six months away instead of the three years in the plan. Fewer trips to the junkyard for you, my friend. That's gotta count for something."

"I know how impatient you are, Meep, and how you like things to happen fast, but..." Holden tried to explain. "Everything's changing lately. Nothing feels...steady. Why rock the boat some more?"

"You know, for once, I think Swinger's actually given this some thought." Tom surprised Holden by lobbying in his favor. "I'm proud of you for considering the consequences, taking it seriously and thinking with your big head even though there's a pretty girl involved. *However—*"

"Shit, Tom?" Holden squeezed his eyes closed and let his head drop back against the couch cushion. "You too?"

"I'm just going to say I think there might be something other than this TV commotion influencing your decisions." The guy wasn't often wrong. Maybe this time he wasn't either.

"Like what?"

"Positive changes don't make an environment unstable. Growing up, none of you had secure lives. I get that. I tried my best, even though our family was unconventional."

"No one's complaining about how things have turned out, Tom." Holden's heart ached. Making his dad feel like he hadn't done his job was definitely *not* on his agenda for today. "You, Hot Rods...saved my life. I'm not complaining."

"I know, son. But things were unpredictable at times. We've all got issues. They'd flare up. Or, hell, just dealing with the lot of you going through puberty at the same time. Jesus. That was rough. The last few months here have been like that again, but with higher stakes. Turmoil's always bothered you most, Swinger. Especially when there are genuine connections at stake. Trust yourself and the rest of our gang. No one's trying to dispose of you. They're not replacing you with these lovely ladies they've found. And if you decide that you'd like what they have, that you're open to a bond with a woman—Sabra or someone else—you shouldn't question your feelings. It's okay. It might work out and it might not, but you'll survive. Just because things are different don't mean they're worse." Tom paused as if considering whether to continue. Then he did. "I felt like you were on edge already. I suspect Sabra might be amplifying that unrest in you. Do me a favor, would you? Give her a chance. Don't assume it's impossible to overcome your biology, okay?"

"He's got a point, Holden." Kaige spoke softly, without a trace of the temper he'd wrestled his entire life. Nola stroked his arm, kept him calm. "You don't have to be like your parents. Your mom, I mean. Nola proved that to me. Hell, I haven't punched anything in days. And look at Bryce and Kae, they're nothing like their fathers. The important stuff at Hot Rods isn't going away. *We're* not. Our foundation is solid. A TV show, lovers, or whatever other bullshit that comes our way won't mess that up."

As Holden took time to really digest what they were telling him, Nola capitalized on the opening. She looked to Eli. "Look, you hired me because you trusted me."

"And in your professional opinion…" Eli winced, looking between Alanso and Sally.

"You'd be stupid not to do this." She crossed her arms.

Holden took a breath, prepared to fight to the death though he knew he was doomed. Hell, he kind of agreed with them. He didn't have the guts to recall his stand though.

Eli interrupted. "I think you both made your cases pretty clear. I'm not going to choose between you or decide this for everyone. We'll vote. But there have to be some parameters. *If* we do this, Kaelyn and Bryce must be excluded. Hundred percent this time. We can't chance breaking our gag deal with the senator. Also, if Holden or anyone else wants to join those ranks—now or at any time in the future—we'll make it a stipulation in our agreement with Sabra. Fair enough?"

Holden nodded.

"Okay, then. Who's for getting Swinger laid by giving his girl good news?" Eli grinned as he rubbed his hands together.

As each person's fingers raised, even Tom's and Ms. Brown's, Holden knew what he had to do. Buck up and be a Hot Rod. He was the odd man out. Even Buster McHightops— their shop mascot—lifted a paw, hoping for one of the treats Rebel and Kae had been rewarding him with during his puppy training.

Holden cursed under his breath, then put his fist in the air. "We're in it together. Just don't say I didn't warn you."

"Then it's settled." Eli smiled, slow and sure, before winking at Holden. "Why don't you take the morning off tomorrow? Go tell Sabra we're in. Maybe she'll be happy enough to forgive you for being such a dickhead."

"Fuck me." Holden groaned.

"If you're lucky, Swinger." Carver smacked his ass when he stood. "She's pretty damn hot."

CHAPTER FOUR

They'd milled about in the kitchen for a while, grabbing beers and shooting the shit about nothing important, reassuring each other their bonds were still strong. Holden smiled with tight lips as Tom clapped him on the shoulder then headed down the open-backed metal staircase toward his house, right across the driveway. Ms. Brown had fled before him and already peeled out of the garage's lot. Swinger wondered what that was about.

As if they wanted to make sure he was okay, the guys huddled around him while they each pulled up a stool at the bar that divided the kitchen from the rest of their massive joint living area.

"Is it the thought of us touching Sabra that's bothering you?" Roman asked, as if he might be more understanding of a jealous streak than the rest of the Hot Rods.

Holden lifted a brow as he considered what that could mean for them. What if

Roman didn't get off on sharing Carver as much as it had seemed now that the two of them had bonded, drawing even closer than their prior best-friend status?

A problem for another day. They seemed to be piling up.

"Nah." It truly wasn't. Kind of the opposite, actually.

"Then what's going on?" Carver asked from Holden's other side. He wriggled his fingertip in Swinger's ear, at least until Holden hauled off and smacked the jerk's forearm away. They might have devolved into a pile of wrestling dumbasses if Holden could have stopped the question playing through his mind.

"Quit that, asshole." He sighed, then asked before he could snuff his curiosity, "What would you do if I wanted to watch you fuck her?"

"I'd drop trou and get to work. Same as any true pal." Meep grinned. "Come on, it's not like you haven't screwed around with the other ladies. You know I'd make it good for Sabra and thank you both for getting me laid."

Carver licked his lips. Roman grumbled something, though not loud enough for Holden to make it out.

"Good." Holden readjusted his filling cock through his pants. "But what about you?"

When he knocked his elbow into Kaige's ribs, the other guy smacked the back of Swinger's head. "Huh? What about me?"

"Would *you* fuck Sabra?" Holden asked.

"Is that a theoretical question? As in, is she hot enough to turn me on? 'Cause, yeah, she's smoking. Likc she's got that total badass thing going despite how cute she looks. It's a certified boner-inducing combination." Nova glanced at his fiancée to see if she minded him telling the truth. "Or are you trying to figure out what the rules are here? You know, like...now that I'm with Nola, what happens during group stuff?"

"That." Holden clenched his fingers into a fist. "If you haven't noticed, we're running out of unattached guys. And it seems kind of...sucky...to change the rules now. I *like* sharing. The girls. You guys. Whoever. I want a woman who's into it too. No holds barred. Or positions."

"Oh." Mustang Sally worried her lip as she considered the implications of his question. "I hadn't thought about swapping partners."

"You've been with the guys lots of times, *chica*." Alanso twirled her hair and chuckled. "Feel free to jump them whenever, even though you're married to Cobra and me."

"But I haven't seen you with another woman since Bambi." She paused. "I'm not sure I could stand it without scratching a bitch's eyes out for pleasing you. And…"

"That's totally not fair." Kaelyn frowned as she finished Sally's thought. "Poop."

"Does that bother you guys?" Nola asked the men ringing them.

"I've got no complaints." Gentle caresses on her shoulder accompanied Kaige's reassurance.

They all looked to Eli. He shrugged, then said, "Why don't we each take some time to think about this, and the possible repercussions, when we're less riled up and able to use some logic? Swinger, I think you should call the Powertools crew soon and get their take on it. I feel like they could give you better insights than we could at this point."

Holden nodded. "I will. Good idea."

He glanced around, noticing the guys' cocks hadn't wilted. In fact, they seemed pumped up by the thought of experimenting, if the bulges in their sweats had anything to say about it. He could relate.

Swinger imagined Sabra surrounded by the Hot Rods. He pictured her laid out and ravished by the guys while he sat back and enjoyed the show. Weird or not, he did have a thing for watching. Would she get off on his laser stare as his friends delivered more rapture than she could stand?

He hoped so.

"Jeez. I think you're going to burst a blood vessel if you're not careful. Quit thinking so damn hard and go with it." Carver hopped off his stool. He glanced at Roman before yanking the back of Holden's T-shirt until he crashed onto the floor. His friends managed to keep him from injuring himself too badly as they each grabbed some part of him and dragged him backward.

"Oomph." Half towed and half crab walking, Holden went where Meep tugged him, to the edge of the area rug. Clothes hit the ground beside him as his friends began to shed them without having to be told.

"Wait." He clambered to his knees, then regained his feet, approaching Kaelyn—the sweetest and most inexperienced of them. If she could handle this, there might be hope. He touched her cheek as Bryce spied on them with eagle eyes. "Just try one little experiment for me. If this sucks, we'll forget about it without involving anyone else. Please?"

She peeked at Rebel, who smiled his encouragement and nodded.

"You've made out with me before, but never Kaige. Why don't you give him a kiss?" Holden nudged the two unlikely friends toward each other. Nola relinquished her grip on Nova's tensed forearm, her brow furrowed.

"Don't worry, there's a consolation prize for you." Swinger distracted Nola by angling her toward Alanso. He didn't want to piss off a pregnant lady—already her hormones were increasing her fierceness to epic proportions. "Same for you. Why not see what Al tastes like?"

"And me?" Sally put one hand on her hip.

"Hey, you've had them all. Get to the back of the line, sis." Kaelyn surprised the friends with her quick retort. Her smile belied any faux-hostility in her accusation.

"You've still got me, baby." Eli slung an arm around Mustang's shoulders and tugged her close.

"Mmm." She smiled up at him before they sealed their lips. And as if that one act spurred the rest of them to join, they did.

Kaige took a final look at Bryce, probably judging the brute's reach, before he cupped Kae's cheek in his hand and lowered his lips to hers for a sweet kiss. She brought out a degree of gentleness in him that Holden wouldn't have believed he possessed. Meanwhile, Nola took charge of her encounter, clutching Alanso's shoulders and mashing him to her before he could protest.

Not that he would have.

She devoured him, as if her passion could burn away any possessiveness that might be stalking her while her fiancé sampled his friend's woman's taste. Alanso growled, then cursed in Spanish before giving as good as he got. He had Nola bent backward over his thick arm in no time.

It was only Swinger's groan that broke the moment. Cursing himself, he wished he could swallow the sound when the oddly matched couples broke apart with a combination of sighs, dazed blinks and obvious arousal.

Bryce tapped Kaige on the shoulder. "I'm cutting in here, buddy."

Kaelyn peeked up at her boyfriend from beneath a curtain of platinum hair. "Did that make you mad?"

"Horny, more like it." He lowered his mate to the floor, where Carver and Roman already had tucked their hands in each other's pants at the center of the storm of pheromones swirling around them like a twister.

"He's a great kisser, Mustang." Nola patted Alanso on the ass and sent him back to his husband and wife.

"Mmm. I know." Sally didn't hesitate in reclaiming her guy. She flung herself at him and wrapped her thighs around his waist. "He's an even better lover, though."

Always eager, the gang seemed to be racing in high gear tonight. Holden caught Bryce's eye as his friend inclined his head in an open invitation to double-team Kaelyn. Swinger decided he'd rather survey the action from his place at the center of the gang's coupling.

Surrounded by lust and shared intimacy, he felt safe, though he'd never admit something so pussified to his friends. The only way it could be better was if he could give that same gift to someone he cared about. Someone cool and sexy like Sabra.

Swinger shoved his sweats down and whipped his T-shirt over his head, flinging it somewhere behind the couch. He reclined so that he was propped on one elbow with his body stretched out on the thick carpet. His free hand wrapped around his cock and worked on turning his half-mast stiffy into a full-blown hard-on. It didn't take long.

Before he'd managed a half dozen yanks, Eli was already buried balls-deep in his wife while Alanso was feeding her his own thick erection. Nola perched reverse cowgirl on Nova's lap next to the trio. Holden jerked when she leaned forward and sampled Eli's parted mouth. The sassy exchange of a quick yet decadent kiss voluntarily crossed the lines they'd artificially drawn.

Kaige pumped into his fiancée harder as he watched his woman use Cobra to get off. The pair grinned at each other when they broke apart, jostled by their respective fucking. Mustang patted Eli's clenching abdomen as he rode her, her own stamp of approval.

Kaelyn had wedged herself between Bryce and Carver, as if searching for something more intense than the gentle loving she soaked in each night she spent in Rebel's bed. When they played together, she got the extra level of spice she'd admitted she craved.

Meep looked around. He spotted Holden alone and abandoned his post. Roman took up where he left off with an intensity that made Swinger wonder if he was concentrating on distancing himself from Carver, just a little bit.

Oblivious to Barracuda's stare on his retreating back, Meep scooted closer to Holden, crawling to eliminate the last few feet between them. Swinger glanced away from the stare Carver leveled at him, afraid of what his friend might see.

He shouldn't have worried.

"We're always going to be here for you. No one's going to come between us. None of us would let that happen. And if you believe us, you should know it's possible to find other people who would say the same thing, Swinger." The guy didn't wait for an answer. Likely didn't want one. They weren't exactly great at dealing with their emotions. Unless it was like this. With raw passion and pure adrenaline. Less talking, more fucking.

Holden cupped his friend's head in his palm and drew the guy's eager mouth toward him.

Warm lips closed over the head of his cock, sucking precome from the tip.

His toes curled, and so did his fingers, tangled in Meep's hair.

Roman did something devious to Kaelyn, which Holden couldn't quite see. Whatever it was had the woman coming within seconds. She shuddered and moaned. Except instead of deflating, her hunger renewed. She dug her nails into Bryce's powerful shoulders and shoved until Rebel rolled to his back and let her use him however she liked.

Not far behind his lover, Roman took advantage of Carver's position on all fours to slip in between the guy's legs and fondle his balls. He raked the fingers of his free hand down Meep's spine, until his hand tucked into the valley of Carver's ass.

Meep's steady sucking stuttered on Holden's shaft when Roman massaged his hole.

Helpful if nothing else, Holden leaned to one side to snag a bottle of lube from the drawer in the end table. He tossed it to Barracuda, then tapped his finger on Meep's cheek. "Watch those teeth when he plows into you, 'kay?"

To be a jerk, Meep nipped Holden's balls before resuming his deep-throating. Too bad for him—Swinger liked it. Even better was the guy's hum as Roman sank into his ass, fusing them before beginning a steady pumping into his welcoming hole.

Holden wrapped his hands around Carver's upper arms, helping to steady the guy and also to ground himself. Free to display his affection for his fellow Hot Rods, he took advantage of the opportunity, rubbing his thumbs over the tattooed biceps that quivered beneath his touch.

Meep sucked harder, laving the underside of Holden's cock.

Cries of completion echoed around the room as their partners found ecstasy. It seemed no one had stamina tonight. At least not for this first round. The tension that had arced between them resolved into calm. Their sharing reassured them that they were okay, their friendship was fine, their bonds were strong. None of them would be alone again, left to fend for themselves in a cold, cruel world even if they didn't always agree.

That thought alone had Holden's balls tightening.

He blinked a few times, trying to clear the stinging in his eyes. Surprised, he flinched when someone touched his shoulder softly. Kaelyn. She smiled at him before kissing him gently. Bryce sat behind Holden and held him upright, so he could simply enjoy the pleasure Carver granted him with every bob of his sultry mouth over Holden's cock.

Sally and Nola came to lounge on his other side. Mustang rested her head on his arm as Nola massaged his scalp and feathered his hair from his brow. Eli, Alanso and Kaige knelt behind their ladies, lending their support and encouragement as Meep devoured Holden and Roman drove them all as he set the increasing tempo for their liaison.

Pumping harder, Barracuda forced Carver to take Holden deeper, which he did enthusiastically. The man could suck cock like no one else.

Still, Swinger held on, refusing to come until each of his friends had been satisfied.

The moment Carver shouted around his mouthful of dick, while Kaelyn snuck a hand beneath him to milk his cock, Roman joined in with fierce grunts. He impaled Meep on his shaft, shooting deep into the other man's ass.

Only then did Holden let go. He kept his eyes open as he came. Meeting the supportive gazes of the people surrounding him with their love. They amplified his rapture until negative thoughts vanished and only bliss remained.

They brought him down gently before pairing off again to cuddle.

This time his solo status bothered him where it never had before. Being part of the gang was all he'd ever known. But maybe it wasn't all he was destined to have.

The thought terrified him.

He tucked his limp cock into his sweats and hastily drew them into place at his waist. What if he'd missed his chance because he'd had blinders on? Was it too late to change his mind about Sabra?

He needed to think.

"You awake over there?" Carver kicked his ribs lightly from where he hogged the sectional sofa. "We're going to watch a movie. The new one with Joe Danger. You in?"

"Nah, I'm beat. I think I'm going to crash." He rolled to his feet and stuck his hands in his pockets.

"Gotta go think of what to say to Sabra tomorrow, you mean?" Alanso poked at Swinger. No sense in denying it.

"I'm going to have to make it good, right?" He winced. Would she bust his balls for the way he'd treated her? He deserved it. Still didn't mean he couldn't hope he got off easy. Maybe if he distracted her, she'd forgive him. After all, he knew how to give a woman pleasure. And he liked doing it. A lot.

"I'd say so." Bryce nodded.

"Right. Well, night then."

"Sleep well." Nola skimmed her fingers over his forearm as he passed.

Swallowing hard, he paused then bent to kiss her cheek. Holden didn't want her to think, for one moment, that there was any bad blood between them. "Thanks for doing what's right for the shop, even if I gave you a hard time."

"I like when you give me a *hard time*, Swinger." She smiled up at him.

"Hey now." Kaige mock-growled at his woman.

She only laughed. "You like it too. Either that or you've got a wrench in your pocket right now. Who wants to bet you don't make it through the movie without having to get off again?"

"Not me. He's gonna do you," Kaelyn singsonged. And everyone laughed.

Holden chuckled too as he entered his room and flopped into bed. Staring up at the ceiling, he attempted to compose a speech for Sabra. In the end, he decided to wing it. To speak from his heart and hope she understood. At least he knew he'd have some time to work on her if they'd be filming the Hot Rods show together for a while.

Despite the thoughts rolling around in Holden's brain, or maybe because the ruckus of the day had exhausted him, it wasn't long before he drifted off, with explosions and the shouts the Hot Rods fired at the screen in the other room keeping him company.

***

Holden managed not to scream this time when a loud bang woke him. It was so dark, he couldn't see the empty soda bottle in his hands—the one he'd dug out of the garbage then pretended was a submarine, zooming around the bathtub he slept in. He wanted to run into the other room, where his mommy lived all the time and he got to live sometimes. But last time he'd gone inside on his own she'd yelled at him and spanked him for making her boyfriend angry. Sitting had been ouchy for days after. He was supposed to stay in the bathroom, on his blanket-bed in the tub, until she came to get him. No matter what, mister.

If Holden didn't be good, the man—whichever one was over to play tonight, he couldn't remember all their names—might hurt him, she'd said. They might hit him. Or worse. He remembered the way some of her friends had looked at him lately, before she'd started making him sleep in the dirty old bathroom. Creepy creepers. They made his tummy ache.

He thought his mommy should have nicer friends. Ones who played whatever games she wanted instead of making her cry after they left, and sometimes before. Holden cheered her up as much as he could, drawing pictures and acting silly. Making Mommy laugh was his favorite game. Except he wasn't always so good at it.

He tied his blanket around his neck like a cape and crawled out of the tub with his Top Secret Quiet superpowers engaged. A sliver of orangey light fell through the crack in the door onto the floor. Pressing his eye to the gap, he peeked into the other room, then wished he hadn't.

Mommy had crashed onto the floor. Her eyes looked funny again, like when she took too much of her medicine. Holden looked around the room, as much as he could through the crack. He didn't see anyone else. Holding his breath, he listened real hard. No one made any noise, except for his mommy, who sounded like she'd run extra fast up all the steps to their apartment.

His hand wiggled the doorknob. Would she be mad if he snuggled by her? That was what she did when he was sick and needed medicine of his own. Even if his medicine never made him feel like hers did.

Holden was scared. Something felt bad. And he wanted his mommy.

He scampered out of the smelly bathroom, letting the door bang. Mommy must be very sick. She didn't yell at him for making noise or hurting the door. He trotted to her and lay by her side, burrowing into her warmth. Tonight she didn't make him cozy, though. She seemed as cold as he was.

"Holden?" she whispered, her voice not sounding pretty like when she sang him songs.

"I'm sorry, Mommy. I don't want to sleep in the tub anymore. Can I stay here with you?" He petted her soft hair.

"For a little while."

He had to lean closer because he could hardly hear her whisper. A lot of times she told him not to yell inside. And at night he had to be quiet as a mouse. So he didn't say anything. The funny sound of her breathing only got faster, even though she was resting.

"What's wrong, Mommy? Are you sick? Didn't you get enough medicine?" He looked onto the table and saw lots of wrappers and a scary needle. He hoped he never needed medicine like that. "Do you need me to get some from the man on the corner? I could go see if he's there or wait until he's not sleeping again."

"I deserve this." She moaned and rubbed her face on the yucky carpet.

"Huh?" Holden sat up, the skin on his neck acting like there were bugs on it. He scratched it.

"Don't let anyone do this to you, baby." She sobbed. "Never let someone hurt you like this."

Tears poured down his mommy's face along with snot. She rubbed them away.

Something red smeared on her cheeks.
Blood.

"Mommy! You're bleeding." He felt sick when he could smell it. On her. On him as he tried to smoosh her skin together like she'd done the time he bashed his shin on the corner of the radiator when he learned flying was only make believe but gravity was for real.

"So sorry. I can't do it anymore, kiddo. If your dad had stuck around, maybe it would have been different. If he'd cared about us—"

"I don't need a daddy. Remember how you told me to tell the other kids that when they teased me? You said it's fine to have just a mommy who loves you very much. I love you too, Mommy. We don't need a daddy." His fingers were slimy with the blood now, but he was too scared to look at it.

"That's right. And you don't need a mommy either, brave boy. You'll be fine without me. Never forget. You don't need anyone, Holden. Stay strong. Stay alone. Have fun, but don't give your heart away. Or you'll never survive. This pain...it's unbearable. Nothing dulls it anymore. Be smarter than me. Don't take that risk. Do you hear me?" It took her a long time to say all those words. But still she managed her mom-voice. The kind she used when he was about to get in trouble. *"Promise, Holden."*

"Okay, Mommy." He didn't really understand what she was saying, but he wanted her not-angry.

"Good boy." She smiled just a little, the first time he'd seen her mouth shaped like anything other than a frown in a while.

It looked weird upside down.

Her lips. Getting gray now.

"I love you, baby." Another tear rolled down her cheek, but no more followed. *"I'm sorry."*

And then she went super, extra, really still. Like she was playing the quiet game in the *bathtub and didn't want any of her friends to hear them. Except she was way better at it than he was.*

He always had to pee or wanted to play.
Mommy was like a statue.
She didn't even blink.
Or breathe.
"Mommy! Mommy, wake up. Mommy!"
No matter how hard he shook her, she didn't.

***

Holden howled again, his raw throat making a pitiful hoarse cry. He thrashed against whatever kept him pinned down, unable to save his mom. Why hadn't he gone for help? Why hadn't he realized she was dying right in front of his eyes?

"Hey, you're all right." Warm hands held him, not the cold ones he'd never erase from his memory. "Swinger, it's me. Carver. Roman's coming too. He went to get you a drink. You're home at Hot Rods. Holden. Can you hear me? Wake up, damn it!"

His heart raced. The sawing action of his ragged breaths made his lungs burn.

Instead of focusing on that, he listened to the voice.

The calm one. The steady one. It had never let him down. Unlike his mom. Or his sperm donor, who'd disappointed them both. Crushed them.

"Meep," he rasped.

"Yeah." The guy loosened his hold as Holden went slack. "Yeah, it's me. Fuck. That was a bad one. You haven't dreamed of her in a while."

"Sorry." Swinger swallowed hard, or attempted to around the dry lump in his throat. "I told you to pick a different room instead of sharing a wall with me. You never would listen."

"I'd rather be close. You'd do the same for me." Carver sagged as he sat beside Holden. He kept his hand on Swinger's shoulder, solid and unshakeable. After one of these nightmares, Holden hated to be alone. Even if he couldn't stand to talk about what he'd relived.

Meep understood and gave Holden what he needed—space *and* company.

Roman crashed through the door, his eyes wild as he surveyed the scene. The pulsing light from the Hot Rods screensaver Holden intentionally left on each night highlighted Barracuda's craggy profile. "Is he okay?"

Roman spoke to Carver, as if Holden weren't sitting right there.

"Getting there." Swinger spoke for himself. "Better if you've got a beer or something for me to chug."

Barracuda didn't speak, his eyes still glued to Meep. He handed over a mostly empty 750 mL bottle of St. George Absinthe Verte. Holden accepted the strong shit from Roman. Why did the guy have this stashed in his room? Was he drinking hardcore again?

Right now, Swinger could only be glad. He downed three gulps—feeling every bit of the 120-proof liquid searing his guts—before handing the poison back. Or he would have, if Carver hadn't confiscated it.

"Thanks," Holden mumbled as he crashed to his back on the bed, his forearm flung over his sweat-drenched brow and eyes so he didn't have to meet their concerned gazes. It'd been years since he had a nightmare that vivid.

"No problem." Carver didn't abandon him. Neither did Barracuda edge toward the door. No, he sank onto the mattress, the heat of his body radiating full length against Holden's.

"Mind if we stay?" Roman asked from his other side. The bed shifted again as he made himself comfy without waiting for a response. Thank God they all had king-sized beds. They had come in handy through the years. Though Holden preferred their other activities to this.

"No." The guys both tensed, so Holden clarified, "I mean, I don't want you to leave. I—uh—I *need* you."

Wasn't that the pisser? His mom had made him swear he'd never get attached, presumably to a woman. He hadn't. But if anything ever happened to the Hot Rods, he'd be lost. Totaled. So how could he consider flirting with Sabra, the only other person who'd tempted him to get closer than a casual, one-night affair?

A problem for tomorrow.

Maybe his ghosts wouldn't look so intimidating in the light of day.

Holden let his head rest on Carver's shoulder while Roman reached across Swinger's abdomen to hold Meep's hand. If that meant Holden's friends' arms locked together in an impromptu seat-belt hug around him, well, he didn't plan to complain.

"Hey, Swinger," Roman mumbled, as if he'd had a few shots of that disgusting liquor himself.

"Yeah?" He didn't look at the other man.

"If you snore, I'm gonna pound your nuts." He grunted, then relaxed on the pillow they shared.

"Wouldn't dare wake you. Obviously you need as much beauty sleep as possible, dude. I swear you're getting uglier by the day."

Holden silently thanked his friend for returning them to more comfortable ground. Maybe now he could rest. Numbness from the alcohol speeding through his veins combined with the familiarity of his friends and their antics to soothe him.

Determined to salvage what rest he could, he closed his eyes and rehearsed his apology to Sabra, allowing himself to be distracted by visions of what might have been if he hadn't walked away to keep his painful past at bay. His mom wouldn't approve.

Luckily, the remainder of the night passed peacefully as his garagemates kept old horrors at bay.

CHAPTER FIVE

"Is your new plan to chase Sabra away by pretending to be a stalker or something?" Carver plucked the phone out of Holden's hand and jabbed the disconnect button on the screen.

"Hey, I'm just doing what you guys asked." He shrugged as if he didn't give a damn when he really wanted to run around the garage at full speed a few dozen times like Buster McHightops did when a squirrel crossed his path.

He'd psyched himself up for a confrontation with Sabra, figuring they could hash out some stuff before they were in close contact daily. Instead, all he'd gotten was her voicemail. About forty times in a row.

Come to think of it, that might look a tad excessive.

"Cool." Carver nodded and buffed the same spot on his project for far too long.

"What?" Holden hated to ask, but the guy clearly had something on his mind.

"You said it goes straight to voicemail without ringing, right?" Meep glanced over his shoulder, his face too serene to be as innocent as he seemed.

"Yeah."

"Well, that probably means she turned her phone off. Or it ran out of juice." Meep grinned as he asked, "Why not head over to her apartment and let her know? Be a good citizen. And while you're there, kiss and make up. Work some of this energy out of your system before you drive us insane."

"Is it that obvious?" Holden turned and banged his head on his toolbox hard enough to rattle his brains. Unfortunately it didn't seem to knock any sense into him. He actually considered Carver's suggestion. "Don't answer that. I guess I just don't get why. Why her? I hardly know her. *Why* can't I stop thinking about her?"

Neither of them dared mention that she'd resurrected his nightmares, too.

"I'm not sure." Carver edged closer. "Chemistry, I guess. The connection is there. Or it could be. Hell, Kaige was kind of like that with Nola. All those emails back and forth when he'd never written as much as a postcard before. Maybe you should find out what's between the two of you before you screw it up. It's after quitting time. Go have some fun. Give her a hell of a ride. Scratch that itch and maybe you'll forget about her by morning. Just make sure she's cool with temporary before you bone her so you don't screw things up with the show. She could make you regret it if you piss her off. Editing can make you look like a tool, you know?"

"Do you think that's okay?" He rubbed the base of his neck, where his Hot Rods tattoo rode his collarbones. "Me hooking up with her?"

"Hell yes. Be safe, like always. Enjoy yourself. And her. Then come home to us when you're back to fucking normal." Carver knew without explanation what Holden had worried about the entire day. None of them had strayed outside the Hot Rods for their affairs lately. There'd been no need. "It's fine, Swinger. We don't own you. No one will be pissed if you get some on the side."

"Are you sure?" He glanced around the shop nervously. The other guys—and Sally—went about their usual business, sliding under cars, painting them, meeting with customers to discuss restomods and ringing people up in the service station. Nola and Kaelyn laughed together about something in the office, completely ignoring his man-to-man moment with Carver.

"Yes. We talked about it at lunch." It was impossible to be pissed when Carver grinned.

"So you drew the short straw, huh?" A laugh bubbled from Holden. He should have figured.

"You got it. Terrible luck, as always," Meep grumbled. "So can we quit this bro-talk?"

Holden didn't find it necessary to inform Carver that the straws were rigged. Meep would figure it out eventually and they'd make it up to him, somehow. It was one of Swinger's favorite running jokes around the shop. He never had outgrown the need to make people laugh. Or at least to try.

He clapped Carver on the shoulder. "Thanks. This is finished. Would you let Bryce know to call the owner for pick up?"

"Sure." Meep nodded.

Holden packed the rest of his tools and tidied his station. Then he stripped off his coveralls, patted his keys in his pocket, and took a few strides toward the gleaming 1969 Dodge Dart Swinger waiting for him out back. His baby could use a quick ride.

"Yo, Swinger."

"Yeah?" He walked backward as he faced Carver once more.

"If you're really smooth, you'll find a way to clear that pile of missed calls from her phone before she notices them." Carver shook his head ruefully. "Otherwise, she's going to know how pitiful you are. Then she'll never fuck you—forget coming home with you—and I won't get to help you satisfy her. Because it's all about me, you know?"

Holden flashed Meep the finger. Still, that wasn't a terrible idea.

Either the call purging or the Hot Rods invite.

If things went well, he'd consider it.

He ducked into the jet-black interior of his Swinger and ran his hands over the new leather he'd wrapped the steering wheel with last weekend. The fancy lacework had taken him hours, but he loved how it had turned out. When he set his mind to something, he usually made sure it lived up to his high expectations.

Untangling this mess with Sabra would be no different.

***

Sabra paused as the roar of a ridiculously overpowered engine neared her apartment. Good thing she'd finished her marathon meditation or the giant raspberry emanating from the approaching motor would have snapped her out of her zone. Damn teenagers and their love affair with pizza.

She went to the window and looked out as the vehicle pulled into the private parking area behind the shop. *Bad move, jerkwad.* Mr. Tortelli routinely had people towed. Sabra liked to think it was because he kept the area free for her and her guests, but his hyper-diligence probably had more to do with his cut of the fee.

Her fingers froze on the window as she prepared to raise it and shout a warning to the unsuspecting driver. Until she saw who climbed from the cherry-red classic granting infinite cool points to her parking lot by association.

"Holden," she whispered.

As if he heard her, he looked up at her window. She jumped, though he didn't seem to notice her in the shadows. Instead, he turned and plucked a daisy from the snarl of wildflowers beyond the pavement.

The pounding of her heart stuttered.

Then he looked down at the perfectly imperfect bloom, frowned and tossed it to the ground. Once he started in her direction, he moved quickly.

Sabra only had a moment to fluff her hair using the hazy reflection on the glass. She winced as she glanced at her workout gear and hoped she didn't stink too bad. Nice. Out of options, she grabbed a lemon from the water bottle she'd kept close while practicing yoga and rubbed it on her neck before taking a sip of her post-exercise drink—the alcoholic kind—as she flitted through the galley kitchen.

Though his knock wasn't overly aggressive, she still jerked in response.

Several deep breaths later, she opened the door and tried to act surprised. "Holden? What are you doing here?"

"I—uh—" He seemed speechless as he took in her sticky state. *That bad?*

She winced until she realized he was staring at her chest.

Sabra clapped her palms over her hard nipples, visible through the soft cotton of her sports bra. Not just noticeable, but obvious. *Damn.* Hopefully, he'd assume it was the reaction of her damp skin as it cooled.

She knew better.

"Whoa." He shook his head then met her gaze, his pupils dilated. "Sorry. Is this a bad time? I tried to call. You weren't answering. I thought maybe you'd like to know your phone isn't working. It kept skipping directly to voicemail."

"Shit! I silenced it." She raced inside, unconcerned when he shut the door and followed her. "I was...concentrating."

"All day?" He tipped his head. "On what? The only time I'm that focused and that sweaty is when…"

And suddenly she knew what gutter his mind had jumped into when he'd asked about his timing. For a moment, she couldn't resist teasing him. Something told her he'd do the same if their positions were reversed. His infectious grin and dimples, which he'd flashed the day of Kaige and Nola's engagement, screamed practical joker.

"When what? When you're enjoying a good lay?" She hummed and trailed her fingertips down her neck, discreetly flicking off some pulp that had adhered to her skin. Smooth. "Boning some lucky girl…or guy…or *both*…until they see stars?"

To her surprise, Holden actually flushed. He didn't deny her speculation about his bisexuality. Damn, that possibility magnified his sexiness, taking it to a whole new level.

His throat flexed as he swallowed hard then nodded. "Should I come back some other day? Or you could call the shop if you want to talk about business. I didn't mean to interrupt. Sorry, it was presumptuous of me to assume it was unintentional when you didn't answer. Freaking Carver and his dumbass schemes."

He angled toward the exit.

"Don't leave," she almost-shouted. "It's not what you think. I was training. I'm a jivamukti junkie."

"Jiva-*whaa*?" His brows lifted and drew together as he tried to decipher her explanation.

"Jivamukti. It's a type of extreme yoga. I use it to tone up while honing my mind. To reflect. It's kind of an obsession, actually. How I wind down. It's probably almost as good as your method for releasing tension."

"I wouldn't go that far. But that's cool." Holden relaxed. He returned, resting his hip against her counter. His innate sexiness filled her humble living quarters, enhancing the effect of the adrenaline zinging through her veins after her epic session. "Does that mean you're extra bendy and stuff?"

"I guess you could say that." An understatement.

His smile turned naughty and his gaze appreciative.

She couldn't help but beam. "If you're nice to me, maybe I'll show you later. Anyway, I just uncorked a decent bottle of wine. I'm not going to lie. It usually oxidizes before I can drink a quarter of it. So you might as well help me toss some back after delivering the bad news."

"Who says that's what I came here for?" He reached over and idly twirled her phone on the counter, fiddling with the screen while she poured a second glass for him. She didn't mind him tapping away on the thing in time to his own beat. Hopefully, he turned the volume up again. She couldn't believe she'd missed his calls.

"Isn't it?" she wondered. During her rumination earlier, she'd allowed herself to visualize for the first time what it would be like if she *didn't* get her way. She'd bounce back, think of some other plan for survival.

"Actually, no." Holden rubbed a hand down his face, drawing her attention to his own pretty-damn-perfect physique. She wondered what he did to stay in shape. Sex burned an awful lot of calories, she supposed. Especially hedonistic orgies.

"Wait, *what*? Are you sure you didn't stop by to crush my hopes?" It took her rational side a moment to catch up.

He laughed. "Yep. Unless you've changed your mind about what you're rooting for."

"Hell no, I haven't." Wine sloshed onto her knuckles as she bounced. "I want to produce a show about Hot Rods. It'll be a smashing success. I can picture it already."

Another of the scenarios she'd visualized over the past few weeks. This one repeatedly.

"Well, you're going to get your wish. Those crazy bastards I work with are egomaniacs. They want to be the next big thing. More famous than the guys on *Pawn Stars* or *Duck Dynasty*, even." He chuckled. "Maybe we should grow beards down to our dicks. Think that would help?"

Sabra chuckled. "Nah. I'm sure they're not your style. But honestly? Are you serious?"

As soon as he nodded, she hurdled the counter. His eyes widened, but he caught her when she flung herself at him. Impressing her with his steady center of gravity—a requirement for jivamukti—he didn't spill a drop of wine when he filched the glass from her yet held her steady, with one arm supporting her waist.

Then again, her legs had somehow wound around him and smothered his hips. She'd climbed him like a koala on eucalyptus.

If he minded, he didn't say so. In fact, his fingers kneaded her ass.

"Thank you." Without giving herself time to second guess her instincts, she leaned into him and kissed him gently. Not the ravenous suck-face kind of making out they'd indulged in the night he'd driven her home from Bad News. But something sweeter, and more genuine.

He dropped her as if she'd farted on him.

"Don't be so damn nice to me, grateful. I voted no." At least he didn't lie to her. Still, the truth stung more than she thought it would.

"Oh." She wiped her mouth as if she could scrub the taste of him from her lips, or her memory. They both reached for their drinks and took a synchronized sip. Okay, more like a gulp.

"And those bastards have stipulations." He took a deep breath, then ticked them off on his fingers.

No Kaelyn and Bryce. *Check.*

Anyone else could choose to be excluded. *Check.*

Nothing went out the door before Eli screened it and approved. *Check.*

Assurance that business, not personal shenanigans, would be the primary focus of the program. *Check.*

"That's great. I can live with all of that." Gripping the counter, she prevented herself from reaching for him again. "We only have about a month of shooting to make the station's deadline. That's isn't a lot to get exactly what I need for the pilot."

"Hang on." Holden slowed her down. "What do you mean?"

"See, I thought of this idea after I heard rumors that the national network is unhappy with one of their primetime shows. Rumor has it that they're scouring local affiliates for a replacement program. Our station doesn't have an offering to submit—yet. They're scrambling for something because it would mean more support from the national level and prestige too. You guys are kind of local celebrities. And the execs know me and the quality of my work down at the station so I won't have to rely on my dickhead old boss for a reference. It should be an easy sell. After the station agrees to take us on as their bid, we can start lobbying for the national network to select *Hot Rods* as the mid-season replacement they're desperate for. Something fresh, original and...perfect. If we hurry, we can be in production in time."

"Does that mean it's not a done deal yet?" Holden asked.

"Oh. Well, I think it'll be a no-brainer. But...I guess the execs could say no to airing you locally. And the competition at the national level will be strong." She frowned. "I'm sorry. I don't think I explained the process well enough. I was really excited...and, frankly, I didn't think there was any chance you would say yes."

"I didn't," he reminded her. And though he didn't say so, he seemed cheered by the prospect that they might not get airtime. "I'll let the guys know about the extra steps, no problem."

"Tha—" She stopped herself this time when she realized her appreciation really would be unwelcome. He seemed kind of annoyed by her happiness. What did the guy have against cheering her up? Hell, giving her the best news of her entire life?

"Shit." Holden tipped his glass and drained the dregs of his wine. "I'm gonna have to drink more if you're planning to be this cute when you're hanging out with us."

"Why?" She couldn't decide if he liked her or hated her. Maybe both.

"Because I'm so damn hard it hurts, and I have been for weeks." The admission startled her almost as much as his hand, which wandered toward his crotch to rearrange the noticeable bulge in his jeans. "You're not making this easy for me."

"I could make it really simple." A glutton for punishment, she sashayed closer. When she went to her tiptoes and laid her palms on his solid chest, she could nuzzle his neck. So she did. Not too tall, he was the perfect height for her. "We're adults, Holden. *Consenting* adults. I've realized lately that I let a lot of opportunities pass me by while I was so focused on my career. I don't want to keep repeating my mistakes. Tell me you won't let a romp screw up our shoot and I'm game for helping you out with that problem in your pants. I've never been this attracted to a guy in my life."

"I should go and keep us both from fucking up royally." His fingers plucked hers from his neck. But instead of releasing them, he lingered, caressing them. She thought she heard him whisper, "What would Tom do?"

Mr. London seemed entirely too responsible for what she had in mind. So she appealed to the impulsive streak Holden couldn't begin to camouflage.

"What fun would that be?" This devilish side had never escaped her before. Something about the mechanic drew it from her, inciting her to break rules. To riot against playing it safe.

"None," he murmured against her lips. "Absolutely none."

And then they were kissing.

His mouth claimed hers, gliding across it with skilled caresses that spoke of a heck of a lot of practice. A low hum, which reminded her of a growl, emanated from his chest as he indulged his wicked tendencies and coaxed similar urges from her.

Funny, she'd never seen the appeal of a bad boy before. Until him. He encouraged her to run wild with flicks of his tongue at the corner of her mouth. Accepting, she opened for him, applying herself to the kiss.

Sabra nipped his lower lip, loving the ferocious need he inspired in her. She didn't have to be careful. He could handle anything she did. The reserve she'd always worn like a cloak fell away, leaving her exposed and open to his explorations.

His fingers edged beneath her waistband before rising again to rake over her exposed abdomen. A shiver ran through her when he traced the fine indentions alongside the muscles she worked so hard for. An appreciative groan flooded her mouth as he curled his hands around her waist and tucked her even tighter to his chest.

Gasping at the full contact, she broke free from his mouth and drew in a shaky breath. He took the opportunity to stray along her jawbone and then down to her neck, sucking at maddening spots below her ear. Lower.

Yanking his head back, he made a funny face. Mouth puckered. "You taste...sour."

"Citrusy?" She laughed, somehow unashamed with him. He put her at ease, something not easy to do.

"Yeah, I guess. Like a Lemonhead. I love those damn things." He licked his lips, then eyed her neck like he might dive in for a second taste.

"Sorry, impromptu deodorant." Why lie? "Didn't want to scare you away at first sniff."

"You saw me pull in?" He smiled.

"More like heard you a mile away. Shouldn't you be able to install a decent muffler on that jalopy?" Abstaining from teasing him would be impossible. They both knew the beastly roar of his engine was intentional.

His laugh thrilled her and made her insides turn squishy. Almost as much as his broad grin. "You gave a shit what I thought."

"Guess so." She shrugged.

"For the record, I like the way you smell. If you haven't noticed, I like pretty much everything about you." He guided her hand to his jeans-clad erection and squeezed.

"Come with me." She drew him down the hall, past her studio. Bamboo screens and foam mats dotted the open wood floor of what should have been a guest bedroom. A water feature tinkled in the corner of her sanctuary.

Holden studied the space over his shoulder as she dragged him toward the bathroom attached to her room. "Wow, you're serious about the yoga stuff, aren't you?"

"Yes." Sabra smiled. "And I was practicing advanced asana—hip openers, arm balances and inversions—for hours before you showed up."

"You do have really great posture. On the news it kind of made you look like you have a stick up your ass, and for some reason that turns me on. A lot." He groaned. "Do you have a pair of glasses somewhere? Maybe you could put your hair in a bun like a naughty librarian or something? Slip into one of those conservative navy suits you used to wear? I'm gonna miss seeing them on the news."

A laugh burst from her. Once she started, she couldn't stop. Tension even her training hadn't erased bled from her as she melted in Holden's arms.

"Never mind. This side of you is sexy too." He teased her hair where it tumbled from her ponytail. "Maybe I should help you loosen up more."

When he swooped in for another kiss, she dodged, knowing she'd never have the willpower to stop him again. "I need a shower if we're going to take this any further. You can wait or you can—"

He stripped off his shirt before they'd made it through the doorway.

"Mmm." She raked her gaze over his defined chest, bare and smooth. Although she'd imagined him with lots of ink, like his friends, she only spotted a single tattoo on his naturally tan skin. *Hot Rods*. Of course.

Which reminded her... "Is this okay? I don't know the rules. I mean, when it comes to your friends."

"The guys and the Hot Rod ladies know I'm here." Holden knelt and stripped off her stretchy black pants, pausing to draw a fingertip over the blue polish on her big toe. "Don't think about them. Concentrate on me."

The unspoken plea in his intense gaze took her breath. She cupped his cheeks and leaned down to kiss him. Too bad if he didn't appreciate affection mixed with passion. She couldn't seem to separate the two around him. *Better be careful*, she warned herself.

Passion and desire erased any hint of discomfort she might have experienced being nude, or nearly, with a man she didn't know very well. Denying the hunger in his kiss, his investigative touches and his searing gaze would have been impossible anyway.

Sabra rested her hands on his shoulders, her nails digging in when their potent attraction threw her the slightest bit off balance, something that never happened. As if to prove it to herself, she stood, whipped her sports bra over her head and tugged at the elastic that had barely restrained her messy ponytail.

She smirked as she walked backward, flicked on her shower, then gave it a moment to heat up. Holden stalked toward her as if he'd press her into the tub and attempt to make love to her while still partially dressed.

"Your jeans?"

"Oh, right." He scowled as he unlaced his boots, kicked them into the corner near her hamper, then worked on his belt. When it hung open, he shoved denim, leather and the soft cotton briefs beneath from his hips all at once. It hadn't taken long for him to get gloriously naked.

Still, her uterus would have drummed its fingers, if it had any.

Sabra pivoted and stepped into the combo shower and tub. Spray hit her chest then her face as she ducked into the refreshing stream of water. Dried sweat, proof of her earlier hard work, sluiced from her body along with some of her nervous energy.

She shook her hair out of her face and slicked it back before pivoting to face Holden. The position, elbows bent at head height, put her breasts completely on display. Without wasting an instant, he joined her and began lapping dew from the mounds, which looked pretty fantastic if she did say so herself. She peeked down at his tongue laving her flesh.

Too much more of that scenery and she'd abandon any semblance of restraint.

Okay, so that had gone out the window around the time she'd launched herself over the kitchen counter at him. If he hadn't stopped them, she probably would have ridden him right there on the hard floor.

Thank God one of them had some sense.

For a woman who prided herself on rationality, his ability to destroy her logic was simultaneously terrifying and freeing.

Sabra decided to focus on the positive aspects of their explosive chemistry when he snagged the liquid soap, lathered up his hands and sank to his knees. As he worked, he nibbled each patch of skin he cleaned, lingering on especially sensitive places like the dip of her waist and her lower belly.

While he entertained his mouth with the light sucking and wet kisses, his fingers began to wander closer to the apex of her thighs. Helping him however possible, she spread her feet, giving him more room to maneuver. Pulses of pleasure contracted her core, prodding her to beg for him to touch her. Fill her. Grant her relief.

Cool tile at her back tempered his flashing heat on her front side as she leaned against the surround. And when he traced her slit, she didn't hesitate, propping one foot on his shoulder with enough fluid grace to make it clear that the motion held no challenge for her.

"Pretty," he murmured as he inspected her closely before applying his mouth to her aching flesh.

Sabra folded her wrists on top of her head, trying to prevent herself from grinding him closer, showing him just how badly she needed him to posses her in some fashion. Instead of sliding his thick fingers inside her, he braced her thigh with one broad and completely unnecessary hand. The other cupped her foundation leg just above the knee, as if she needed his assistance to hold her pose.

"I'm not going to fall. Promise." She whimpered when he swiped his tongue over her clit. "Please, I need something inside me."

"If I do this right, you'll be dizzy." He winked up at her.

"Are you kidding?" Sabra wiggled her brows and relished his laugh, which buffeted her activated nerve endings. Amusing him thrilled her, maybe even more than his touch. "This is nothing. If you want to see a cool trick, give me a couple inches here. Don't want to knock one of your teeth out or give you some crazy sex injury."

"I'd rather stay close and give you a couple *other* inches." His smoky timbre inspired a shiver that raced up her spine. Still, she didn't get that many chances to show off her skills. And his grin was infectious. He appreciated her playful side and she liked flaunting it for once.

Without grabbing her foot, Sabra lifted her leg first to waist level, then higher, her hip joint rotating without complaint. When her knee brushed her cheek, she looped an arm around it and prepared to hold the position for as long as it took.

All those stretches were finally paying off.

"Holy shit." Holden stared, his face level with her very spread, very open, very wet pussy.

"Are you going to look at it all day or do something with it?" Though she teased, a rush of pride surged through her at his blatant appreciation.

"I could fuck you so damn deep like this." He grimaced. "Just not while fooling around in the shower. I don't want either of us to die like that. Happy, but embarrassing. The guys would put it on my tombstone for sure."

"So stop chit-chatting and get me off. Then I'll show you a better position on the nice soft carpet in my bedroom." She couldn't say what possessed her, but she buried the fingers of her free hand in Holden's hair.

"Yes, ma'am. Though I'm doubting you can top this masterpiece. Unless you have a secret twin in your closet or something." His chuckle muffled against her drenched flesh as he buried his mouth in her folds. Her toes curled high in the air.

The man knew his way around a woman's body, that was for sure. Allowing herself to benefit from his expertise, she settled into the moment and his intimate touches. He prodded her opening until the tip of his middle finger sank inside. Water ran across her neck and down her body, raining over him as well.

Nothing deterred him from seeing to her rapture.

He worked himself inside her slowly yet relentlessly until he'd penetrated as far as his digit would allow. She spasmed hard enough to crush his finger when he lapped at her exposed clit, though still she needed more.

"Holden." Her plaintive moan had him glancing up without stopping his efforts.

"Let me take it slow. You're so damn tiny. Tight." A groan snuck between his clenched teeth. "I don't want to hurt you."

"It already does." She shook her head when he began to withdraw. "I mean...

Wanting you this much. I've never needed someone like this."

It shouldn't have surprised her. Weeks of lusting after the guy had her primed and ready. Beyond desperate. She'd worry about that later. For now, there was no room for embarrassment beside her raging lust.

"I've got you," he promised.

Though trusting didn't come easily to her, she believed him.

When she relaxed, her leg drew even tighter to her face, spreading her to the max.

"Damn." Holden introduced a second finger to her greedy pussy and then another. All the while he continued to tease her clit with circular flicks from the tip of his tongue. When he tapped a particularly electric spot inside her, she wobbled, her leg dipping a fraction of an inch.

True to his word, he supported her, refusing to let her sway despite her shift. He braced her, counterbalancing her as if they'd practiced pairs jivamukti for years instead of coming together for the first time moments earlier. Once she steadied, he drilled deeper, unrelenting in his pursuit of her rapture.

Knowing he could read her so easily, so thoroughly, pushed her over the edge. No one had ever gotten her like that before. Not without having to be told.

Sabra bent her supporting knee, grinding onto both his pumping hand and his massaging mouth. The combination of the dual pressures increased in tandem, driving her over the edge into climax.

Colors burst behind her scrunched eyelids. In Holden's iron grasp, she flew higher than she'd ever gone before. Still, she knew with him they could reach even greater peaks.

When she could concentrate on anything but the rapture pounding through every inch of her body again, he'd stood up. Hugging her to him, he lowered her leg gently, keeping her from melting to the bottom of her tub and swirling down the drain.

He grounded her, steadied her and held her close as she recovered.

Together, they stood in the cooling raindrops until her pulse returned to halfway normal.

"Better?" he whispered into the soaked hair at her temple.

"Mmm." A soft moan answered for her. Sabra couldn't help herself. She licked the side of his neck, close to where her mouth rested naturally with her head on his shoulder. Granting herself permission, she allowed her hands to roam over the hard planes of his body and the valleys between his sculpted muscles.

He held her as if she weighed nothing, displaying some strength of his own.

Could he go all night without stopping to refuel?

Sabra decided to find out. She had nothing to lose, since she'd already shown him how frantic she was for him. "Better, but not perfect—yet. More."

She stopped just short of pleading.

Looking into her eyes, he seemed to weigh her request before nodding. "Thank God. Me too. I need to feel you around my cock. I want to be buried in that sexy little pussy. I'm going to fuck you until you can't take any more. Neither of us can."

Sabra bit her lower lip and peered up at him through lashes dotted with water drops. She prayed he made good on that promise when she gave him a slight nod.

Cursing under his breath, he lifted her from the tub onto the soft mat beside it then hurriedly soaped himself. She stared at the suds as they slid down his gorgeous form, wishing she'd taken the chance to pamper him as he'd done to her.

Later. Much later, she hoped.

Holden looked up and caught her staring. One corner of his mouth kicked into a grin that had her squirming. She cupped her own breast, pinching the nipple as if it were his mouth suckling her again. With a clatter, the soap dropped forgotten to the tub floor. Water cut off when he wrenched the valve closed and hopped the low tub wall.

Windmilling his arms, he skidded, then righted himself before wrapping his hand around her wrist. He tugged her into the bedroom, then fused their mouths. Damp bodies slid against each other as they writhed together, lost in the storm of arousal that coalesced around them again.

Would it be like this every time they touched? Intense to the point of frightening, the rush elated her.

"Are you laughing?" he asked brokenly between kisses.

"Kind of." She gulped for air. "Can't. Believe. It."

"Same here." Holden smiled at her, tucking a wet strand of hair behind her ear before smacking her ass, dispelling the tenderness that threatened to sprout in their intimate silence. "Show me some of these tricks of yours."

He gripped the base of his cock and stroked, making her knees weak at exactly the wrong time. She glanced at the thick shaft poking between the ring of his fingers every time he glided to the base.

"Oh no." He shook his head. "I won't last two seconds if you suck me. It's getting iffy as it is. Come on, Sabra. Put your moves where your mouth was. Or…well…shit. You know what I mean."

At least she wasn't the only one befuddled by their attraction.

Teasing him did wonders for her self-esteem. As best as she could, she watched his eyes go wide when she planted one foot on the floor and dipped forward with the other leg extended straight behind her in an arabesque. Arms out, she balanced as her back leg rose into full-split position, completing an advanced version of the Dancing Shiva pose, natrajasana.

From where Holden stood, rooted to the floor behind her, he had a clear view of the most private parts of her. And easy access too.

"Don't move." Awe painted his command as he scrambled for the bathroom. From the rustle of denim, she assumed he raided his jeans, probably for a condom. She hoped for protection since she'd completely ditched responsibility along with rational thought.

"Perfect," he murmured as he circled her, running his fingers along her taut muscles as if he appreciated them rather than being intimidated by them, as some guys were. Meanwhile, he rolled latex down his steely erection, preparing to enter her and satisfy them both.

Sabra moaned.

"Is that uncomfortable?" His head tipped to the side as he approached her from behind. "We can take this to the bed. I don't need anything fancy. Being inside you will be enough. Plenty."

Quickly, she shook her head, erasing his concerns. How could she explain that the discipline it took to maintain her position only added fuel to the conflagration of need inside her? Without direction, he seemed to understand. Or maybe he simply couldn't wait another second.

Same as her.

Holden aimed the blunt head of his cock at her saturated pussy. As soon as he notched inside it, he cursed. Unless that was her. Either way, he reached forward and grasped her hands, which were spread out on either side of her and slightly behind, like the wings she would need to soar.

With his unshakeable hold, he drew her closer, impaling her on his cock.

"Yes!" she screamed as he filled her inch by inch, taking full advantage of her flexibility to drill her to the max.

"That's right. Take all of me, Sabra," he snarled as he lodged inside her, his balls tapping her clit as they swung forward with the momentum caused by the impact of their torsos slapping together.

One of her legs tucked against his and the other drew a line from his pelvis up his chest, her knee resting somewhere near his shoulder. He turned his head and nipped her shin as he began to rock, receding a bit before plunging deep once more.

Using their unwavering grip as leverage, they set a rhythm all their own. Perfectly in sync, they drew apart then came back together, each time with a bit more power. Holden tunneled within her, forcing the rings of muscle trying to constrict around him to stretch and accommodate his impressive girth, which she swore continued to plump up as he impaled her over and over.

The motion had her breasts swaying beneath her, increasing the tug at her center that ramped her higher with each thrust. Before she was ready for the bliss of their joining to end, ecstasy built within her again, so intense that she knew she couldn't resist for long.

"Go ahead, Sabra," Holden rasped. "Come on me. I want to feel you shatter around my cock."

As if she could resist his dirty talk.

The next time his balls tapped her clit, she lost the battle, succumbing to mind-numbing pleasure. Yet through the haze of rapture, she didn't hear his answering cries. In fact, he stopped moving altogether instead of ramping up the intensity of his lunges.

"You don't think I'm done with you yet, do you?" He chuckled when her stiff spine loosened and she understood that he meant to keep fucking her. Give her more pleasure than she'd dreamed of. More than he already had. "You're not the only one around here who knows some tricks."

Holden began to move once again. The motion rejuvenated her orgasm, sending sparks along her nerves and igniting her passion once more. He fucked into her hard enough that he nudged them both forward.

Sabra wriggled her fingers free of his grasp. She braced her hands on the floor and grinned over her shoulder at him. "Don't hold back on my account. Here, is this better?"

When she rotated her hips, his cock slipped free and nudged her mound on his next pass.

"No, definitely worse," he griped.

Until she kept her forward momentum, going into a handstand. Then she bent her knees. He took the cue, stepping into the embrace of her legs, which wound around him like a boa constrictor that hadn't had a decent meal in years.

Come to think of it, she hadn't. Not if this was what it felt like to feast.

Holden wrapped his hands around her waist, his thumbs nearly touching in the small of her back. He drew her to him, hardly allowing her to hold any of her own weight as he plowed into her. Ass bouncing on his abs, she rocked to his beat, taking all of him and helping him nudge the wall of her pussy with the thick cap of his cock.

Right. There.

Again.

And again.

He fucked her until her eyes crossed and they both sounded as if they'd run a marathon, their breaths loud in the quiet apartment. As she felt herself climbing toward the summit of her pleasure, she knew she didn't want to crest without him again.

More than the physical release Holden could grant her, she wanted the emotional closeness of sharing the experience with him.

"H-holden," she stuttered as she attempted to gain his attention.

"Yeah?" The monosyllabic response had her certain he concentrated to keep his own rapture at bay. Exactly what she didn't want.

"Let go. Come with me this time. Please. Show me how much you like it." She would probably hate herself later for adding, "Me."

A roar left him as his willpower fled. He jackhammered into her, moving fast and furious—if not far—on each stroke. The precision of his spearing hips directed his cock to the place she loved it most. She stood no chance. Hoping the wringing of her pussy was enough to trigger his orgasm, she surrendered.

He cried out her name as she gave herself to the moment, and to him.

Thrilled, she felt his shaft thicken, the veins caressing her swollen flesh and adding another dimension to the cacophony of sensations swarming inside her. Heat burst from her core as he pumped into her, spraying his release into the condom that constituted the only barrier between them.

Sabra concentrated on milking him dry, hoping she imparted a sliver of the joy he'd given her. Arms shaking, she sighed when he lifted her, supporting all her weight and his even as he erupted within her. He stood, with her legs clasped backwards around him, his chest pressed to her back and his arms around her middle.

When they'd finished quaking, he carried her to the bed and tipped onto the mattress with her. Their bodies stayed connected as they recovered, his frame covering hers. Protecting her and smothering her with his warmth.

"I think I'm going to need another shower," she mumbled.

Holden laughed, rich and deep, the sound making her happy places tingle even more than the proper fucking he'd given her. "I'll take a hundred a day with you if they all end like that."

CHAPTER SIX

"Jesus, Sabra." Holden flopped onto his back and drew her to him, arranging her like a blanket over his chest. "I can't believe we just did that. It was so fucking good. I hardly know you and we wandered straight into circus freak territory."

"It felt right," she admitted, though her cheeks turned a pretty shade of salmon. "I kind of assumed you were no stranger to stuff like that. I was playing it cool to keep up with you. At least one of us should have some experience in hookups considering how easy—and not awkward—that was. Besides, it seemed like you were enjoying yourself."

"Seriously? Is there any doubt? That was in no way a complaint." He nuzzled her neck, thrilled when shivers ran up her spine, her nipples scrunching where their bodies pressed together. "You were spectacular. And so is whatever this is between us. Irresistible. You're not pissed, are you? I usually at least take a woman out to a nice dinner before we get to the down and dirty. I couldn't help myself. And I'm so glad I didn't. Believe me, the only time it's ever been that a-*fucking*-mazing is..."

It didn't take a genius to figure out what he'd almost admitted. Sabra was no dummy. She guessed, "Is when you're with the Hot Rods?"

"Yeah." He refused to meet her gaze, staring instead at the serene ink drawing, which hung on the wall opposite her headboard, of a monastery in the mountains surrounded by tiered farmland. Time for some levity. He didn't do serious with women. Or anyone, really. "Please tell me you don't mind if I brag about you. In detail. Especially about the contortionism. They're going to be so jealous."

Her shy smile did funny shit to his gut when he caught sight of it in his peripheral vision. "Sure, go ahead. I'm not going to lie. Your friends are hot and I don't mind them thinking I deserve to be with someone like you."

"What's that supposed to mean?" He tipped his head, frowning at her implication. "I don't know you that well, but everything I've learned...and seen...and felt, I liked. A lot."

At first he didn't think she planned to respond, and when she did it wasn't a straight answer.

"I guess I have a lot of respect for people who work their way to something from nothing. If it makes you feel better, I don't think we're as much strangers as you believe. I wonder if that's why I felt this instant connection to you and why I don't regret—" She sighed and he'd bet she was remembering how hard and how many times she'd come for him, surrendering completely to their passion. He was. "Well, anyway, we have kind of a lot in common."

Holden held his breath as he waited for her to recant her mumbled confessions. Disappointment zinged through him at the thought of her denial. Certainly not because he cared, but because it *had* been phenomenal.

Instead, silence lingered.

When she didn't backpedal, he focused on what seemed important to her although her dewy skin tempted him to distract them both from somber topics by practicing their freak show tricks.

"Like what?" He shifted, relaxing as his fingers combed her damp and snarled hair.

"For starters, we're both adopted." The click of her teeth after she blurted the factoid made him wonder if she'd meant to spill that juicy secret.

"You are too?" He levered onto an elbow to peer into her eyes. "Wait, how do you know I'm—?"

"Journalist, remember?" A grin tugged her mouth upward as she pointed to her smoking rack. At least until she realized he didn't share her amusement.

Why had she reminded him? Was this a heart-to-heart or some kind of twisted interview?

"Yeah." Holden crashed onto her pillows once more, deluding himself into believing she gave a shit about him personally instead of as some footnote for her show. "So you have the dirt on my mom?"

"No." Sabra hesitated as if she chose her words carefully. "I didn't dig into records that weren't public and accessible. Your juvenile documents are protected. I know about Tom London, though, and his family. Their work with the shelter. And there are newspaper articles about how he took you in—all of you—after his wife died. I wouldn't have been doing my job if I hadn't checked that stuff out."

"That better not be pity I hear." He counteracted her pats on his chest with a snarl.

"Not from me." It didn't seem like a lie, especially when she smacked his abdomen for the thought alone. "You found a good man who built a strong family for you. There are *so* many kids who aren't half as fortunate as us."

He didn't ask her to continue, but he stayed quiet, hoping she'd spill more.

"I don't remember much from the time before my parents—the real ones, not the birth ones—found me." If his arm snaked tighter around her shoulders, they could chalk it up to post-sex snuggling, right? Trapped against him, she nudged his biceps with a hint of a shrug. "I was three when they discovered me playing with a toy pony in the corner booth of the restaurant they own. They hunted for my parents, thinking they'd be frantic with worry over losing their daughter. Clearly not, though. More like they pulled an epic dine-and-dash."

"Ah, damn." Holden knew better than to waste meaningless words on trying to erase the hurt of abandonment. He held her tighter and rocked them both in time to his pounding heart.

Swallowing a few times, she continued. "After a while, they gave up. Officially adopted me when I was six or seven. They never have treated me like anything other than their own kid. My dad says it was fate. My mom says I liked her cooking so much I never wanted to leave. She's right about that."

Sabra offered him a smile. It was weak, though genuine.

Whether the afterglow of their superb sex or this surreal connection between them lubricated her vocal chords, he couldn't say. Still, he'd bet his lucky wrench that she told him things she'd never spilled before. So he zipped his lips and let her get it all out. Vent.

That was what he would do for one of the gang.

"It's weird, you know? My parents are my world. I'd forget I was adopted if they weren't so different from me." She did beam then. He understood why, as he thought of his own deliberate family. No oopsies there. They'd chosen her. Like Tom had picked him.

"How so?" Holden rubbed her back, slow and gentle, drawing circles on her as she confided in him.

"Well, they're kind of homebodies. I like to travel. And they're very...content...with their small-town ways. I've always been super ambitious." Tears prickled her eyes and he felt like shit guessing she scrambled to avoid thinking of the position she'd lost. In part because of him.

"Shit, I'm sorry, Sabra." He rested his forehead on hers. "I know you did your best to keep your promise. And while I'm having a hell of a time with you, I can't help but wish we hadn't run into you that day in the park."

"Then none of *this* would have happened." She wiggled her finger between them. "I have to focus on the new opportunities blossoming now."

Holden admired her resilience. "I'll do what I can to make up for my part of the shitstorm."

"You're a great diversion so far." She winked at him and squirmed a bit, aligning them more completely. Practically purring, she seemed to shake off the clouds over her head, then jumped back to their previous train of thought. About the differences between her and her family. He followed right along, totally in tune with her reasoning. "Plus, you know, my parents are Italian and I'm Asian-American."

Holden grinned, glad to talk about something happier. Tears in a woman's eyes—hers doubly so—were a dangerous weapon that had the power to destroy his defenses. "I like the way you're made. You seem delicate on the outside, but you're fierce on the inside."

He traced her cheekbone then easily encircled her wrist, where it rested on his sternum.

"My dad calls that my warrior spirit, courtesy of my heritage. Randomly, sometimes, I'll be looking at something and know the word for it in Khmer." She rolled her eyes. "It's weird, but I'm used to it."

"What's that?" He squinted as he concentrated. "*Khmer*?"

"Oh, it's the language people speak in Cambodia." Sabra smiled. "I guess that's where my biological parents were from. Or maybe just one of them. No one saw who came into the restaurant with me that day."

"Is that why you like living up here? I swear I can smell pizza every damn time I breathe. Not to mention all that crashing from the kitchen. How do you ignore that when you're getting your Zen on?" Holden idly traced spirals on her spine with the tip of his index finger. His stomach rumbled and they both laughed.

"I never thought about it, but I guess so. It reminds me of home. It's weird how we do stuff like that and don't even realize what a big impact our parents have on us. Our upbringing. Nature versus nurture junk." When he didn't respond, she shut up.

He could have kicked himself for squelching her honest rambling.

Until she came clean, ruining everything.

"Holden?" Her voice quivered when she called his name. The thready sound had his cock perking up.

"Give me a few more minutes to recover. Five, tops." He massaged her hips, hoping she wasn't too sore after he'd practically tied her into a pretzel as he fucked her senseless. Himself too.

"Not that." She giggled as she poked him in his abs. "I wanted to say I'm sorry."

"What for?" He couldn't think of a single thing she should apologize for. He'd never been this content or satisfied. Something about lying here with her sated him. In a way not even sex with the Hot Rods had. He might have freaked out about that if she hadn't ripped his attention away from the stray thought.

"For lying to you." Sabra nibbled her lip when his gaze winged to hers.

"About what?" *Please, don't fuck this up for us.* He'd let himself enjoy her too much. She was going to rip him apart and he knew it from her meek tone and the nip she gave her swollen lower lip before continuing.

"I do actually want to put some social commentary in the Hot Rods show." She glanced away as he sat up in a flash, disentangling them as if she were a poisonous snake instead of a lovely bedmate.

"We're not signing on to be some exhibit in America's TV-land zoo!" At his roar, she flinched. Too bad. Her betrayal cut him unexpectedly deep. He'd started to like her. Not only the cute reporter, but the woman beneath the face on the news. "We do what we do for us, no one else."

"I'm not talking about your sexuality." Sabra's spine stiffened as she prepared to fight. If they'd been in a ring, she'd have been taping her knuckles. Her determination turned him on. She wet her lower lip with the tip of her tongue as she noticed his rejuvenating hard-on.

He whipped a sheet over his crotch.

"Then what?" Holden steeled himself for treachery. Why should it hurt so much? He'd only just met her. Fucked her once. He could walk away at any time. Should. Right then.

Sure.

"I want to highlight the benefits of adoption. Show some of the good work Mr. London has achieved through the shelter and his love for you guys, plus Sally. It's an important issue to me and I think there's enough meat in the garage to keep people interested while saying something meaningful too. Why not do both?"

"I—" Holden opened his mouth then closed it with a snap. Never had he imagined that was her angle. And try as he might, he couldn't see any harm in it. Publicity for the shop *and* the shelter. It couldn't get much better than that.

Unless people saw the relationship they weren't planning to advertise and used it as a black mark against the foundation. Shit. They could end up doing more damage than good if people mixed up the two issues.

"So, this…" He sliced his hand through the air between them, finally realizing why it had been so fucking good. So easy.

Because it hadn't been real. She'd been buttering him up.

And it had worked.

"Hmm?" Sabra glanced up at him with lazy ease he might believe if he hadn't understood how people used sex to play each other. To get what they wanted only to leave their partners behind after they'd sucked them dry. He remembered the pain in his mother's eyes as she bled to death in his arms. After last night's dream, it was hard to forget.

He swallowed compulsively.

Holden wrenched free of Sabra's reaching hands, her warm sheets and the spell she'd woven around him. He rocketed to his feet beside the bed. "This was all some ploy to grease the wheels? To make me let down my guard? Did you expect me to cry for the cameras when we talked about our pasts? Screw you."

"I may be a failure as a newshound. Washed up before I'm thirty. Hell, a lot of things...but I'm *not* a whore." She climbed to her knees and chucked a pillow at his head. "I slept with you because I wanted to. Because there's something crazy between us. I shared more of myself with you in one afternoon than I have with my boring ex-boyfriends in years. And I should have known better."

Holden doubted it was healthy for a person to turn that shade of red.

It bordered on purple.

Another pillow flew at him and then another. She launched them all without pause. Why the hell did one person need so many anyway?

"Get the hell out of here, Holden, if that's what you believe." She wrapped herself in the comforter, then marched to the bathroom and retrieved his soggy clothes. They torpedoed at his neck, his jeans flopping over his head.

He wasn't sure what to think anymore. Memories of his mother and the clients she'd taken assaulted him. Carver too had done unspeakable things to survive. Had he forced Sabra to sleep with him to get something she needed? It hadn't seemed like it when he'd sunk into her moist pussy, but who was to say you couldn't enjoy something you had to do? Past and present blurred. History either tainted what could have been a bright future or saved him from repeating his mother's mistakes. He wasn't sure which.

Either way, he needed to get out of here. Away from everything that had happened and the emotions Sabra amplified in him. Otherwise he'd be having nightmares for weeks. Even Barracuda didn't have enough liquor for that.

"Fine." Holden hopped into his pants while he headed for the door. He didn't stop to contradict Sabra or erase the doubts in her pretty walnut eyes. For every molecule that wanted to hold her and beg forgiveness, a dozen implored him to run before he wounded them both lethally.

"I'm not going to can the show just because you're an asshole!" she shouted after him. "I'll be there when the shop opens in the morning."

Despite himself, he chuckled, with one hand on the doorknob. He stomped into his boot, not bothering to lace it before letting himself out with a final bellowed, "Fine!"

***

127

Holden stormed through the common area of the Hot Rods apartment. He practically tucked and rolled to avoid the barrage of questions, catcalls and curious stares from his garagemates. He was in no mood to deal with their inquisition, no matter how well intended.

"You're not going to tell us how it went?" Mustang asked as he blew past his friends.

"Does she have mutant lady parts or something?" Roman asked, to give him shit.

Carver joined in. "No, she must have seen how damn many times he tried to call her today and laughed his pathetic ass out of there."

"Seriously, dude. Was it that bad?" Kaige shouted at his retreating back.

"Worse. It was fucking perfect." Holden slammed himself into his bedroom and refused to come out when Eli shouted his nickname, Alanso called him a coward in Spanish and someone else followed up with chicken bawking. Surprisingly, it sounded like Kaelyn. They'd obliterated her finishing school manners in record time. He smiled a bit despite his foul mood.

Holden stripped, pausing long enough to sniff his own arm, which reeked. Not of BO. Or grease, for once. Nope. He smelled like Sabra's minty jasmine soap and whatever fresh-scented detergent she'd used on her sheets. A hint of her musk mixed in, giving him an insta-boner.

He flopped onto his bed, his erection slapping his belly as if pissed at him for abandoning the wild woman who'd seemed more than willing to sate his lust. Again. Probably repeatedly. In any number of outrageous positions.

Until he'd jammed his size tens in his mouth.

Each mile he'd driven away from her had filled him with doubts. Had he overreacted?

The Hot Rods had stopped goading him to return to the living room for barely a minute when Holden's laptop went nuts on the distressed wood nightstand beside his bed. He grabbed the computer and hauled it into his lap, hiding the brunt of his nudity from the camera. Though usually he did exactly the opposite when he heard this distinct notification.

The roar of a circular saw blasted from his speakers.

The Powertools were calling.

Sicced on him by his supposed best friends, Holden figured. Damn them. Okay, some part of him found comfort in their concern. Mostly, though, he'd felt like pouting for a while. With a dash of beating himself up thrown in for good measure.

He considered ignoring the crew. Yeah, right. The saw revved again as the ringtone renewed. Almost as loud as one of the engines Alanso rebuilt daily.

They wouldn't be easily dissuaded. Those bastards.

Holden flipped open the lid of his laptop and connected the videochat. "Yo."

"Put on a shirt. This isn't *that* kind of call, Swinger." Neil, one of the guys in the Powertools crew, was uncharacteristically serious as he looped an arm around each of his lovers—Devon on one side and James on the other.

"We figured you wouldn't be in the mood for playing around tonight." Morgan peered into the screen, her face bulging when she got too close to the fish eye lens on their camera. Holden sighed. He hadn't confessed to the Hot Rods, but it'd kind of become a habit for him to observe the Powertools crew during their sessions lately. If he jacked off while riveted to their passionate exchanges, none of them seemed to mind. Something about watching their sharing, genuine concern and caring...okay, fuck it, *love*...turned him on. Big time.

It broke the rules his mother had engraved on his soul when she died. Abandoning him as surely as she'd been forsaken herself.

They lived dangerously. Loved recklessly.

And he'd been along for the ride vicariously.

"Eli mentioned Sabra. What happened tonight? How can we help?" Kayla, another of the crew wives, wondered aloud. "Tell us about her."

"She's adorable, even more tiny than Devon over there, but tough. There's some kind of inner strength—a calm—about her. Most of the time she stuffs her personality inside and comes off very matter-of-fact, like when she's on the news. It's fun to make her laugh. To see what's behind that mask. Her smile—the real one, not the plastic TV one—is killer." Holden thought back to their time together this afternoon. Or even the day they'd spent in the park. "And when she looks at me with those bright, fiery eyes... It does something to me."

He shook his head, wondering if it was possible to be a bigger sucker.

Nope, probably not.

"You have a talent for making people around you happy, Swinger," Devon praised. "That's a good thing."

"I guess." He shrugged. Sometimes it meant no one took him seriously. With Sabra, it felt different, though. Like she appreciated his humor and embraced it without discounting him.

Then again, he could be imagining that. They'd shared a single superior fuck and a few stolen hours together, some of which she'd spent plastered.

Still, he'd been with enough women to know chemistry like theirs was rare.

"I'm still waiting to hear the problem in all this." Mike, the crew's foreman, tapped his chin.

"I guess part of me thinks it's too good to be true." Holden looked away from the family on the other side of the screen. "Being with her is like going all in on your first hand of a poker tournament, you know? So when she told me she wanted to use the Hot Rods show for a political agenda earlier, I felt like I'd taken a bad bet. Fell for her bluff."

"She's going to dig into your sex lives?" Morgan practically growled.

"No, she wants to highlight the power of adoptive families."

"Aww." A few of the crew wives sighed together.

"What's wrong with that?" Joe, Morgan's husband, asked.

"Nothing." He shook his head. "Now that I can think straight, I'll admit it's a good idea. Tom will like it too. It's just that I didn't expect her to spring that on me. And it freaked me out. I believed her when she told me she wasn't going to play us. Maybe I didn't pick up on it because I was so damn focused on other things. On her."

"What we have here is a clear case of commitment phobia." Joe grinned as he ribbed Holden. "You like this girl. Sounds like she blew your mind. Among other things. So what did you do? You went and jammed a wrench in the gears of whatever you're building before you could get going too fast. Classic bonehead move, dirtbag."

"Look. You don't understand." He swallowed hard.

"About your mom?" Mike took the lead effortlessly, transitioning to seriousness. "Actually, we do. Carver is worried about you. All of the Hot Rods are."

Holden gritted his teeth to keep from saying something he might regret. He trusted the crew almost as much as his own gang. Shit. Wasn't that a problem?

"And if you didn't love them, you'd be knocking some heads together right now for spilling your secrets," Dave pointed out. "So when are you going to realize that there are all kinds of relationships out there and that you're already involved in a bunch. Life sucks sometimes. That's true. Look at Tom or Ms. Brown or any of you guys. You haven't had it easy. But loving people and losing them hasn't driven you to the same extremes your mother opted for."

"You can take a free shot for this next time you see me," James volunteered with a wince. "I'm going to just say it. Your mom took the weak way out. You aren't like her. You would fight. Yes, it would suck if you gave your heart to someone who didn't deserve it, or someone who got stolen from you. But you would live. You've already proven you're a survivor, Swinger."

Morgan reached out and pressed her hand to the screen. Holden matched it, silently thanking her for not asking him to respond immediately. At least until he'd swallowed the knot in his throat.

"Hun, I'm sorry to tell you that you're already screwed." She smiled softly as she teased him. "You love those Hot Rods of yours. Buster McHightops too. That booger chewed your favorite jacket to smithereens and you only laughed. Hell, you might even love us a little too. It's why you get off so hard when you watch us."

He nodded.

"So why not admit there's room for one more person in your heart?" Joe asked. "If Sabra's special, if she's making you think about this shit for the first time in your life, I think you should give something more serious than a single afternoon of fucking a shot. Unless it really wasn't that good."

"It was. Great." He drifted off as he remembered how perfectly she'd hugged him. "But, guys, you're forgetting something. That was just her and me. Who knows if she'd be up for anything with the gang? And...well...you know what I like. She'd have to be an exhibitionist to survive around here. What are the odds of that? Slim."

Mike cut him off with a wave. "Eli said she knows about your bond. Doesn't she?"

"Yeah." He thanked the stars for that anyway as he remembered the night Nola had discovered the secret Kaige had kept from her. It had turned out okay in the end—hell, she'd gotten pregnant about twenty minutes later—but what if it hadn't?

"And?" Kate raised her brows.

"She seemed curious." He shrugged, unable to believe it could be more than that. Acceptance. Interest, even. Though... "She even said I could tell the gang about what we did today. Brag about her. You guys, she's unbelievable. Into this crazy kind of super-yoga. Jiva-something."

"Jivamukti?" Kayla seemed impressed. Figured the naturist and natural healer would know all about it.

"Yeah, yeah, that." Holden forgot what they'd been talking about and rambled on. He gushed about Sabra, her flexibility and each of the ways she'd rocked his world earlier.

"Well, there you go." Dave smiled at his wife, Kayla, then back to Holden. "She's open to kinky shit. Cool with your friends and how close you are. Your girl just needs you to show her what she's missing. I bet if she works that hard on her conditioning, she'd be proud to show off the results to the guys you trust so much. Or maybe even *with* them while she lets you watch. It sounds like she wants to impress you. And it's working."

Holden couldn't respond because every drop of blood in his body had rushed between his legs. His balls ached at the thought.

He tuned in again to hear Joe ask, "What do you have to lose?"

"I don't know anymore. Everything is inside out. I see you guys and the rest of my gang... For the first time, I'm starting to wonder if I've had everything backwards."

"You have, dude." Dave didn't mince words. Someone smacked him and he shrugged. "Sorry, but it's true. I'm not saying I blame you. I get why you're screwed up, but it's time to look at the world around you and reevaluate."

"So I really fucked things up with Sabra, didn't I?" He scrubbed his eyes with his knuckles.

"No one can say for sure but her." Mike took charge. "You'd better get some things straight with her quick. For starters...how does she feel about you having sex with the rest of the guys if you're going to be getting it on with her regularly? Is she cool with you fucking them when she's not around, or does she want to be included at first? And how would you feel about them touching her, even if you're not there? It's important to spell shit out when you're working on something this complicated. Whatever you two decide is okay, as long as you agree."

"That's the thing," Holden let his head thunk against his headboard. "I *want* to watch her with the guys. I want to know any woman I bring into the group would be happy and satisfied. I'm just not sure the guys will do it now that they have wives and fiancées and crap."

"Oh." Joe rubbed his chin. "Have you told them that?"

"Yeah." Swinger sighed.

"And?" Kayla asked.

"We haven't tried swapping partners yet. At least not for more than a taste. And now that I've started this solo thing with Sabra, I'm not sure it's right for me to mess around with them. I kind of don't want to unless…"

"Unless she's there with you guys?" Kate's eyes widened. "Wow. You're serious about her if you're considering being exclusive already."

"I know. I'm screwed."

"Well, maybe not yet, but you could be." Devon wiggled her brows. "You do know we're kind of swingers too, don't you?"

"Really?" Holden couldn't ever remember seeing the Powertools crew mix things up. "I mean, I've seen all kinds of casual touches between the whole bunch of you, but never anything blatantly sexual."

"Yep." Neil nodded vigorously. "We have a deal. A birthday bargain."

"Don't tell me that." Holden rubbed his crotch, hoping they couldn't see. "Especially now that I'm never going to get lucky again. I was such a tool. I left her there. Naked and warm and smelling good."

"You're an idiot, Swinger." James shook his head. "That's for sure. If you need inspiration, we'll show you. Your palm might not be as good as your girl, but a little relief could go a long way in making you less of a dipshit. Besides, what are friends for?"

"Don't take this the wrong way." He cleared his throat before announcing, "I think my days of peeping on you guys are over. At least until Sabra's here to watch with me."

"Just a sliver of proof, then. 'Cause now it's killing me that the next birthday isn't for a month." Joe winked at his wife before turning to Kayla and cupping her cheek in his palm.

The other woman smiled up at him before licking her lips, then parting them.

Her husband groaned as another man sealed his mouth to hers and gave her one hell of a kiss. Holden blinked rapidly as he soaked in their shared passion. Meanwhile Morgan and Dave held hands, knowing their turn would come soon.

When the mismatched couple finally broke apart, grinning, Holden had nearly gone insane with lust. Could he really have something like that. Open. Shared. White-hot.

"Focus for a minute, Swinger." Mike broke into his whirling thoughts. "There's another angle to consider. You're so worried about your mom's warning. When are you going to realize that a polyamorous relationship helps, not hurts? Unlike your mom, Sabra—or whoever you pick to join you—would have the protection of all the Hot Rods if something happened to you. Or the other way around. You'll never be alone."

Holden rubbed his temples as he considered the advice.

Dave picked up where Mike had left off. "It's true. There were times after my accident when I was in the hospital that I didn't know if I would ever open my eyes again. Or honestly, if I wanted to. It hurt so much and I thought I'd never be whole. But I always had security. No matter what happened to me, Kayla would be safe. She'd have the crew to lean on."

"I'll tell you this, Swinger," Kayla cut in. "Everyone handles grief differently. I thought I'd go crazy when I saw Dave teetering on the brink of giving up. But even if...even if we'd lost him, I'd never regret a second of loving him."

Dave hugged his wife to his side.

"It's not worth sacrificing a life of happiness, however long—or short—it might be, because you're afraid of losing it," Joe chimed in, adding his two cents. When his son tottered over to his side of the room, Joe bounced Nathan in his lap, playing with the kid's adorable pudgy hands. His mini-bestie, Abby, wasn't far behind.

Holden figured that went twice as much for a parent. Having a child would be awesome and terrifying at once. Still, he couldn't deny the contentment and pure bliss on his friends' faces as they huddled together, one motley family.

He took a deep breath. Then another.

Finally, he nodded.

"I'll try my best." He sighed. "Hell, I might have lost her before I really had her anyway. After today—"

"You're a charming fucker, Swinger." Mike, the crew's foreman, took a slap to the arm from his wife, Kate, for dropping the granddaddy of all curses in front of his toddler daughter, who repeated her idol like a parrot.

"Fooker, winger!" Abby shouted, laughing as everyone stared at her with wide eyes.

"Welllll, looks like we'd better be going," James proclaimed as he, Neil and Devon got to their feet and edged toward the door. "I think I just remembered I had some laundry to do or a grandma to call or something."

The rest of the crew nodded and scattered, none of them ashamed to flee in the face of Kate's wrath. Holden cracked up, safely two states away.

"Laugh now, buddy." Mike groaned. "When you're in my place someday, I'll return the favor."

"Thank you," Holden whispered before disconnecting. And he meant it.

CHAPTER SEVEN

Sabra beamed as she concluded a segment about a rust bucket that had rolled through the big bay doors of Hot Rods—okay, the guys had pushed it inside with an impressive display of tattooed muscles. It had come in moments after she'd arrived for her first day of filming. The first project she'd be able to document from start to finish.

Perfect timing.

Nola had welcomed Sabra and helped her get her equipment set up while showing her mock-ups of the plan for the car. If they could pull off a doozie of a transformation like that, they deserved every bit of the high praise in the referral section of their website. To Sabra, the hunk of junk appeared unsalvageable, but the guys practically drooled as they stood around it with their hands on their trim hips and tossed out ideas for improvements.

Already their well-oiled friendship jumped off the screen. Anything she shot captured it as a byproduct, though she was careful to make sure it was *only* camaraderie she recorded. Since she'd opted for an intimate reality feel, Sabra had decided to do the camera work herself on handheld equipment. Editing and post-production she could handle at night. Saved budget and kept her presence less intrusive. Plus, working solo gave her full control of the show. Win-win.

Her degree in film and journalism certainly would come in handy on this project.

It also let her get up close and intimate, as if she were one of the gang. So she'd spent some time shooting the 3D design Nola had worked up to illustrate the improvements they planned for their new project, then moved on to filming the intake and first bits of work on what Kaige and Bryce swore was a classic beneath centuries of grime.

Secretly, it disappointed her that Holden hadn't been the one waiting for her in the office with one of his patented smiles and an apology for freaking out the day before. He'd already had half his ultra-sexy body stuffed under a vehicle by the time she'd arrived, precisely on time. If he wanted to play it cool like that, so could she.

Except when she stopped filming, he seemed to appear magically beside her. She sensed him, every cell in her body drawn in his direction as if he had polarized her at a fundamental level with the shockwave caused by their epic release.

Instead of the bliss they'd shared, she focused on his rejection to anneal her spine. Otherwise, she'd melt into a puddle of motor oil at his feet.

Holden cleared his throat.

Before he could breach the awkward silence, though, Carver interrupted.

"Hey, Sabster!" Meep called from across the garage. At least he had the decency to wince when he spotted Holden hovering nearby and realized how bad his timing was.

"What the hell do you guys have against using someone's name?" She put her hands up and shrugged. "You know, the one on their damn birth certificate."

Holden grew still next to her. Probably he was thinking the same thing she was. She'd never actually seen her birth certificate. He placed his hand in the small of her back and rubbed lightly. Wasn't he pissed anymore? Maybe he didn't think as badly of her as he'd made her believe. Or he was gallant enough to tend to even those who didn't deserve his kindness and protective instincts?

"I always knew Sabra was my name. I guess it's burned into you by the time you're three," she said low, for his ears only.

"Hell-ooooo." Meep poked her in the ribs, drawing her attention from Holden's soft stare. Hell, how had Carver gotten there so quickly? He really was fast.

"Yes?" she and Holden asked at the same time.

"I had a cancellation after lunch. This dumbass is free too. Care if we fool around with your car a bit? Tune her up?" He wiped his hands on a rag and she felt bad for snapping at him.

"Sure. It's the—"

"I know which one it is." He smirked.

"What? I parked my car in your lot once, for five minutes, and you can pick it out of a lineup? What'd Holden do? Put GPS on it?" She narrowed her eyes at them both.

"Nah, I noticed the distinct scratches on the bumper the night I picked him up from the pizza shop. To us that's as good as a fingerprint." Carver winced. "Please, let me make your car pretty and shiny again. It hurts me to see it dinged up like that. Especially if it's going to sit in front of here for days on end. It's bad advertising for the shop."

She had a feeling he was playing her, but she wouldn't deny him if not doing it caused them trouble. "Sure. Do you have an estimate for the work?"

"We'll talk about that later." Holden shushed her with his fingers over her lips.

Until she bit him. Not *too* hard.

While Carver clutched his side and howled, she clarified. "For the record, someone backed into my car while it was parked and I was inside the grocery store. I'm a good driver. Don't go thinking I crash into stuff at random because I'm a chick."

"If they dared to be that stupid, I'd have ripped their balls off and stuffed them up their tailpipes years ago." Mustang tossed the barb over her shoulder as she passed by wearing a paint-speckled jumpsuit.

Holden gave his hand a few more jiggles then turned to face her. "I assume that means you're still pissed over last night?"

"Pretty much." Honestly, she loved seeing him again, even if she had to pretend she didn't to survive today and every day after.

"Can I talk to you *in private* for a minute?" he asked, shooting Carver the finger.

"Only if I can film an interview with you for the introductions." She shrugged.

"Ug. Fine." He grimaced, then shrugged. "Let's go."

Sabra followed him as he left the garage and circled around behind the building. An open-backed metal staircase led up to the second story, where the Hot Rods lived. She expected him to let her inside, but he never seemed to do what she thought. Instead, he veered off to the side of the landing then up the next flight of narrower steps.

"Uh, is this safe?" She tried not to look through the lacey metal risers as they ascended to dizzying heights. Or maybe it was being in his presence that had her off balance again.

"Trust me." He smiled over his shoulder at her and kept climbing. "There's a great view up here, and no one will bother us."

As they finished their hike, she hit the record button on her camera again. Why not get some great footage and force him to complete her interview before they got into personal territory? When she spied what awaited them she was glad she'd snagged the shot.

A rooftop deck stretched out before her. Slate pavers were ringed by shrubs in black and chrome pots. A pergola covered in flowering vines shaded some areas while chaise lounges were positioned to take advantage of the unobstructed views. From here, she could see all the way to Middletown. Black-and-green-striped onion fields stretched to the mountains on the horizon opposite the cityscape. She panned from east to west, taking it all in.

"Wow." Impressed despite her nervousness over their impending conversation, she peeked around the recreational haven. A bar on one side, plenty of places to relax, read a book or have some other fun in the sun on the low daybeds. There was something for everyone.

"Thanks." He smiled as he snagged a couple bottles of water from the bar fridge, then led her to a comfortable seating area. If the flashing red light on the camera disturbed him, he didn't act like it. She zoomed in on his handsome face, admiring the hint of his dimples up close. "We worked hard on this. Mustang likes to sunbathe up here. Too bad for her, she was doing it on the day Google Earth came around. I think she holds the record as one of the top ten attractions in the state these days."

Sabra shook her head, wondering if he was testing her. Would Sally really want the world to know that? Was it even true? Holden loved playing pranks. She could picture him tricking the viewing audience into searching for something that wasn't there.

Thinking about the sudden popularity of the garage on the map site nearly had her chuckling behind the camera. She loved his sense of humor, even if she didn't plan to admit it.

"So, how long have you guys been in business here?" She steered them back on track.

"Tom opened the service station when he was in his early thirties. Over time, it's grown into the operation you see today. The shop used to be straight maintenance and body work until Eli took an interest in restorations in high school. By then the rest of us guys and Sally had found our way here...home...thanks to Tom and the foundation his wife started before she passed away. We sort of never left." He shrugged. "And I can't imagine ever going now."

"What do you enjoy most about Hot Rods?" She swallowed hard when his eyes flashed and she knew exactly what he was thinking. A vision of tangled, sweaty limbs and ripped male muscles filled her mind. The picture on the screen wobbled as a result of her distraction.

He treated her to one of his full-on smiles, complete with dimples. Damn.

"I guess I like the friendships the best. And getting to make things whole again. Some of the piles of crap that come in here seem worthless. Everyone's given up on them, thrown them in the dump. But we can take them and put them back together. Fix them. Find them new homes with people who will appreciate them. Love them and take care of them. I guess that has a certain appeal to a misfit like me." When he finished speaking, he glanced away, picking at the label on the water bottle he clutched between his knees.

Her heart broke for him.

And a little for herself too. Why hadn't her parents wanted to keep her?

Sabra shut the camera off with a snap. "I'm sorry, I didn't mean to get so personal on record."

"Don't you get it? That's the problem with this whole idea. Hot Rods *is* personal. The garage, Tom, the gang, Buster and Ms. Brown... They're everything I have. Everything that matters, anyway." He scrubbed his hands over his face. "Besides, if you're not digging up dirt for the show, why do you give a shit?"

"After last night I probably shouldn't." She shrugged and started to rise. It had been a mistake to come up here with him and expect...well, anything, really. Hell, she'd been the one to suggest they screw around, no strings. It wouldn't be right to cling like plastic wrap, no matter how desperately she wanted another taste of the wounded man in front of her.

"Ah, shit." Holden abandoned his outpost. He perched beside her on her chaise, refusing to let her go. "I'm sorry, Sabra. You screw with my mind. Not on purpose, I know. It's just that I want you. And I like you. A lot. More than I should."

When she angled her face to read the truth in his eyes, their mouths nearly met.

He could have kissed her. It almost seemed like he would when he leaned a bit closer.

But he didn't.

Instead he whispered, "I have issues. Because of my mom. She *was* a whore. Or at least she let men fuck her for drugs. I'm pretty sure that counts."

"Oh, Holden." Without thought, she wrapped her arms around him and held him tight. Close.

"Shh. Don't stop me now or I won't finish. I've never told anyone except the gang. And then only because..." He paused and looked down at her as if whatever he said would change how she felt about him. "I, uh, have nightmares sometimes. Bad ones."

She squeezed him.

"Thanks, Sabster," he croaked, borrowing the nickname Carver had bestowed. "But could you ease up before you crack a rib? You're pretty strong for a girl, you know?"

This time she didn't hesitate. She let go and punched him in the biceps.

"Ow." He rubbed the spot in mock outrage.

Then they were both grinning, despite the serious conversation.

"That's better." He hummed as he tucked her against his side again. "Anyway, she was messed up because my sperm donor broke her heart and took off. She had to lug around a kid and for a while she was a serial-dater, trying to land a replacement guy. When that didn't work out, well, she kind of went pro."

"Damn." Sabra couldn't imagine what that would do to a child. To his perspective on the world. On relationships. Things were starting to make a lot more sense.

Patient, she found she wanted to do what would make things easier for him. The urge to be with him spiked. Not just physically, but like this, lending support and taking it when she needed some in return. If that meant they had to redraw boundaries, and ensure his comfort, she could handle that.

What they were starting to build felt real. Not a cookie cutter relationship that could be easily defined but something unique and theirs alone. That was enough for her.

"Look, Holden." She took a deep breath, then started talking. "I don't know what the hell happened between us yesterday, but I liked it."

He choked on the sip of water he'd been mid-swallow on. "Uh, good. Me too."

"And despite the fact that you acted like jerk, I kind of want to do it again. Okay, I *really* want to. That's not something I've typically considered before. You know, a fling. But you tempt me to try stuff I used to be afraid of."

If she had expected him to cheer, she missed the mark. He scowled. "So you're not going to demand some kind of girlfriend/boyfriend thing? Or that I only date you? Quit the gang cold turkey?"

"No." Sabra shook her head. As much as she might enjoy such an arrangement, it didn't seem fair. She'd slept with him knowing about his bond with the Hot Rods.

"Oh." Why did he seem kind of disappointed?

"Why am I starting to feel like I can't win with you?" She sighed.

"Probably because I'm twisted up inside when it comes to you." He grimaced. "I'm sorry. Again."

"Don't be. I think I'm going to have to learn to untangle your knots instead of yanking the ends of your strings if we want this thing to be anything other than a disaster." A tremulous smile curled her lips.

"What if I told you I want to try something serious? A real relationship, however we define that." He took her hand in his. "I may totally suck at it."

"I might too." She rubbed her thumb over his knuckles. "But I'd really like to give it a try. With you."

"To be safe, why don't you record me groveling and then we can play it back forty times a day to save time and effort?" He dropped his forehead on her shoulder. "And P.S., yanking anything of mine is probably not the way to go if you want me to calm down."

A laugh burst from Sabra's chest. He had a way of clearing the air with his jokes, making her feel like everything would be okay. Right then she knew he'd survived horrible things by battling them with a positive attitude. Refusing to let the world know how deep it cut him or how scared he might be by laughing in fate's face.

And she wanted to be like him.

Resilient.

So she hooted. Delighted that she'd found someone who could make her feel so much, so soon, and that even if they ended up crashing and burning, he'd be sure to show her things she'd never allowed herself to experience before.

"Damn, I love when you laugh." He stared at her so intensely she feared he might laser a hole through her. "Do it again."

"What?" She did chuckle at his absurd request, though it held a tinge of awkwardness. "I can't do it on command."

"Then I guess I'll just have to tickle you." He snaked an arm around her.

Sabra bolted to her feet before he could pin her in place.

Holden stalked toward her.

She retreated with an equal number of measured steps.

"No. No way." She grinned at the infectiousness of his mischievous side.

"Yep. Definitely." Holden pounced while his lethal attractiveness distracted her.

She dodged his grasping hands and ran for the other side of the roof with him hot on her heels. Cracking up the whole way.

In fact, she laughed so hard, she lost her lead, and he took advantage, tackling her onto the chaise near some potted plants by the stairs to the elevated garden. He straddled her, both of them suffering a fit of hysterics while he tortured her with wriggles of his fingers over her ribs.

The power of his thighs around her waist made her remember how effortlessly he'd supported her while he drove inside her the night before. And she wanted to feel it again.

"Mercy, mercy." She panted between peals of laughter.

"Hmmm." He leaned down and put a kiss on the corner of her lips. "What will you give me if I stop?"

"If you quit it, I won't have to knee you in the nuts." She gasped when he tickled her harder for her insolence.

"Not good enough." He winked as he teased more laughter from her.

When she couldn't catch her breath, he gave her another reprieve.

"Okay, fine. How about a blow job?" She raised her brows.

Holden jolted, then swallowed hard. The bulge growing at the front of his coveralls proved he liked her bribe. "Right now?"

Sabra hadn't really intended the level of naughtiness warranted by midday nookie at her jobsite, but she couldn't deny he tempted her. More than anyone else ever had. She shrugged as much as the weight of him on her would allow.

Without further hesitation, Holden unzipped his coveralls and shrugged out of them. Beneath, he wore a T-shirt with the Hot Rods logo, including all the mechanics' names. It hugged his chest and reminded her of how it had felt to snuggle into him after their session the night before.

Next he fished beneath the hem for his belt, which he unbuckled in a hurry.

This time when Sabra suffered a riot of giggles, he paused. "Um, Sabster? That's not usually the reaction I get when I take my dick out."

His chagrin only made her shoulders shake harder. "Oh my God, my side is broken."

"Here, I'll distract you." He shuffled upward on his knees until they locked beneath her arms. From here, she could see exactly why women and men alike were more likely to hum with approval when they caught sight of his impressive equipment.

She'd been too focused on getting him inside her the day before to explore sufficiently. Today, she had no intentions of repeating that mistake. Taking him in hand, Sabra measured his length with steady strokes of her lightly clasped fingers. She pumped him from root to tip a few times, appreciating how he continued to lengthen and fill out in her hand.

With a smirk, she reached into the open V of his jeans to cup his balls. He hissed and leaned forward, granting her better access. She loved that he trusted her, to put himself so fully at her control. Though she lay under him, she had all the power.

When she raised her head to lick the tip of his cock, he grunted.

Her mouth had barely closed around the smooth tip when someone shouted from the garage below. She froze with his cock poking the barest bit between her parted lips.

"Don't stop now, Sabra." He urged her forward with a sure grip he'd taken by burying his fingers in her hair. Supporting her neck, he urged her to feast on his erection. "The guys are downstairs, working. They don't know or care about us and what we're doing."

A stray thought crossed her mind. What if they did?

This time she opened wider and invited Holden deeper into her mouth. The taste of his precome inspired her to taunt him, suckling as she took more and more of him. There was a lot to fit, but she wasn't about to complain.

"Damn, that's good," he growled above her. "What has you so hungry? Maybe it's the thought of the rest of the gang?"

His question sounded more hopeful than accusatory.

Granting him some relief, she increased the suction on his shaft and fluttered her tongue along the sensitive underside of his cock head. She hoped the gesture communicated more than her greed for his body.

"Really?" He didn't miss her signal. "You like the idea of the guys knowing what we're up to? Maybe I should text one of them to come up here and see how hot you are in person?"

Holden drew his phone from his pocket, cradling it in one palm. He swiped his thumb across the screen. "You'd better tell me now if this is some kind of fantasy that's hot to think about but not one you actually want to bring to life."

She smiled around his shaft, taking all of him this time.

He tossed his head back with a gurgle of delight.

"Swinger?"

Both of them froze, then broke apart in a hurry.

"I swear I didn't send that message." Holden's stare whipped to hers as he tried to stuff himself into his pants. Not for his sake, but for hers, she was sure. Boot steps on the metal stairs approached. "I was only teasing you. Or maybe testing you. I didn't think you'd be ready for that yet. If ever. I'm not trying to pressure you. Just wondered what you thought. If you'd thought about it at all yet. Being together, there are possibilities... I didn't plan to force you into those situations, though. Not so soon, when we're still figuring things out."

"I believe you. For the record, you were turning me on." She discreetly wiped her mouth on the back of her hand as Carver crested the deck.

"Are you serious?" Holden asked, brushing the pad of his thumb over her damp lips.

She didn't have time to respond before Carver joined them.

A single look at their flushed faces and Holden's half-dressed state and Meep knew the score. He pivoted on his heel and made to leave. "Oh, shit. Sorry. Sorry. Just call me Captain Interruptus today. Son of a bitch."

"Meep, it's fine. Come here," Holden called to his friend.

"I should have realized there'd be make-up sex involved in this discussion." Carver slapped his forehead. He slowly turned as if checking to see that they had all the important bits covered.

Sabra took Holden's proffered hand as he helped her sit up. She didn't let go. Instead, she clutched his fingers. Her panties dampened as she looked at Carver in a whole new light. What would it be like if he watched her have sex with Holden?

The glimpse she'd snuck in her mirror last night had reflected some pretty hot loving. They weren't bad looking, either of them, and they worked out like crazy. It turned her on to think of a witness to that passion. Narcissistic? Yeah, kind of. But she took a lot of pride in her body and the hard work it'd taken to get it the way she preferred.

Holden glanced down to where she practically crushed his hand in hers. He whispered, "Are you sure?"

She nodded.

"Meep, you little bastard. Today's your lucky day." He grinned at his partner. "I want to show you something."

"What?" Carver tipped his head, looking around as if they'd hidden a new ride somewhere on the roof.

"The finest woman you'll ever lay eyes on," Holden answered.

"Better not let Sally, Nola or Kaelyn hear you say that." Sabra slapped his ass. "I'd like to count them as friends, not enemies."

"All right." He refined his statement. "The finest woman you'll ever see that you haven't already fucked."

Meep snorted then tried to cut himself off mid-laugh, as if afraid of insulting Sabra with the crass assessment.

She didn't mind. The lady Hot Rods *were* gorgeous, each of them in their own way. And knowing they'd each gotten a piece of the studs roaming around downstairs made her a teeny bit jealous. Some catching up might be in order.

The opportunity to tease them was too good to pass up, however.

"Better not let Ms. Brown hear you say that." Sabra deflected with humor. And was rewarded.

Both Holden and Carver groaned, and not in a good way. Meep said, "Aw, gross, Sabster."

Holden stuck out his tongue and scrubbed his eyes while making a distinct *blech* sound. "I need brain bleach now, babe. Don't get me wrong, she's hot for an older lady, but she's kind of like our mom around here. There are lines even Hot Rods don't cross."

Sabra only laughed.

And soon that was enough to have Holden's full attention on her and the focus back in his eyes, which reheated as he admired her.

"I should punish you for teasing us like that." His voice rang with command that her body secretly wished to obey.

"Now you sound like Roman," Carver mumbled under his breath. If his shifting from foot to foot, accompanied by a squeeze to his groin, was any indication, he didn't exactly mind.

The appreciation in the pair of their gazes infused Sabra with courage. She didn't wait for Holden to strip her. Instead, she bent forward, easily grabbing her ankles then spreading her legs. Her pleated skirt was short enough to show the hint of her ass and the shadowed valley between her legs to the guys. She knew because she'd checked it out this morning before deciding to be bold instead of falling into her old work wardrobe.

She'd figured she'd be safe when even the extreme maneuver only flashed a bit of her private parts. Now it came in handy.

"Wow." Carver watched as Holden approached her. "You really *are* flexible, aren't you?"

"This is nothing, Meep." She winked as she used his nickname. "Ask Holden about last night, if he hasn't told you already."

"Don't worry. I heard about it in enough detail to sport wood at breakfast this morning." Carver rubbed his abdomen restlessly.

"I told you I planned to brag about you." Holden stepped closer and ran his hands along her upper thighs until he cupped her ass in his broad palms.

She rocked into his touch, giving both men a better view of her pretty underwear. After all, she'd worn them especially for Holden. He should get to enjoy the sight of the ruffled boyshorts.

"You're a showoff, aren't you?" He bent at the waist, surprising her with a nip on the thickest part of her ass muscle.

"Takes one to know one," she replied and ground onto the finger he used to trace her slit through her panties.

His laugh mixed with a moan. "Damn. I don't think I've ever had so much fun fucking someone before."

"Technically, you're not fucking yet." Carver sounded as if he gritted his teeth. "I could help you out with that if you want, Holden."

"Just so you know...what he means is that I'm more of a voyeur than an exhibitionist." Holden knelt to bury his nose between her legs and breathe deep. "If I had a second condom in my wallet, I'd let Carver show you how much it turns me on. But no way am I missing out on this tight, hot pussy." He snuck a finger around the elastic of her underwear and into her slippery channel, testing her readiness.

"So get your dipstick in there and check her oil already." Carver unglued his feet from the ground and trotted in front of Sabra. He perched on the end of one of the chaises in front of her and shoved his jeans down his thighs.

She lifted her head enough to watch him curl calloused hands around his cock and start jerking it. "Hell, I might be a voyeur too. Who knew?"

Holden laughed at them both, the rich sound of his chuckle turning her on even more.

But when he tugged her panties off and the head of his cock nudged her opening, she gasped. Need replaced amusement. "Put it in me, Holden."

"We kind of skipped a few steps here. Are you sure you're ready for me?" he asked as he caressed her lower back.

"Stop torturing me and give me your cock. Please." She hated that she begged, but her insides quivered in anticipation of his length stretching her again.

"Give the lady what she wants, Swinger." Carver encouraged his friend as he stroked himself idly, just waiting to rev himself up in time to the pace they set.

Without further debate, Holden tore open the condom he'd grabbed from his wallet, rolled it down his length, then situated himself at her opening once again.

The tip of his cock burrowed inside her.

It wasn't enough.

Sabra flexed, going onto her tiptoes to engulf his hard-on with her pussy. She shoved backward, lodging him inside the tight rings of muscle that cried out in welcome at the reintroduction of his perfect girth.

Holden took the hint. He glided into her depths with one long thrust, then reached down, lifting her torso so he could wrap his arms around her and nuzzle her hair even though he wasn't nearly as limber as she was.

"I swear we'll do this right later. For now, I need to fuck you." His thrusts were sharp and deep when he punctuated his promise.

"From where I'm at, it looks like she wants it just as bad." Carver fisted his cock and began to work it in earnest. None of them were going to have enough restraint to endure this pace, this intensity, for long.

When the force of Holden's fluid drilling shoved her forward, Meep used his free hand to brace her for his friend's invasion. Again and again, Holden breached her. His cock pressed on all the right places inside her and before she could warn him, she shattered.

The orgasm surprised her, never having come so easily in the past.

She'd simply enjoyed and it'd happened. No thinking. No trying. No self-control.

So unlike her.

And she never wanted it to end.

When she came, her half-lidded stare flicking between Holden over her shoulder and Carver in front of her, his hand flashing over his cock fast enough to make her sure she knew why his nickname was Meep, she spasmed harder than she ever had in her life before. It was no coincidence Holden gave her the best orgasm of all time as his friend looked on.

She could get used to the Hot Rods.

As if he couldn't resist the milking of her pussy, Holden grunted. He wrapped his hands around her hips and clutched her to his pelvis as he buried himself completely and let go. His own climax pulsed through him, his seed pouring into the latex separating them. She wished she'd told him she was on birth control.

Even more arousing, though, was the sight of Carver's come erupting from his cock. If she hadn't been shaking as if the whole garage had suddenly been hit by an earthquake, she might have leaned forward and tasted the fluid that shot from his erection in pump after pump.

"I think he liked that," Holden rasped against her neck in between hot kisses and tender nibbles. "So did I. You're amazing. You know that, right?"

"Hell yes, you are, Sabster." Caver flopped to his back on the chaise as he caught his breath.

Her pussy still periodically squeezed Holden when he sighed and slipped from her clutches. Weak knees led to her perching on the corner of Carver's chair.

Before things could get weird, he tucked his softening cock into his pants, adjusted himself then kissed her cheek. "I'm going to go back downstairs so you two can talk some more. I promise I won't interrupt again."

"What if I want you to?" She couldn't believe she'd asked. Her cheeks heated as she peeked at Holden for his response.

A contented grin stretched across his face. Thank God.

"You know where to find me." Carver bussed her cheek before murmuring, "Thank you for trusting us. Take it easy on Swinger, would you?"

Unexpected tears pricked her eyes, so she nodded instead of replying.

When Meep disappeared down the stairs, Holden gathered her to him and arranged them both on the chaise, where they snuggled together. A luxury she probably couldn't afford if she was going to accomplish her goals and capture Hot Rods on film.

Damn.

She pried herself from his grip, hating the tiny gap between them. "I need you to understand that I'm serious about the work I'm doing here. We shouldn't..."

"Fuck on the clock?"

She nodded.

"Agreed." He winked. "I'm not usually irresponsible when it comes to business or my partners. Besides, that sounds kinda painful, huh?"

Sabra laughed, delighting them both. "Sure does. I have no desire to have a minute hand up my ass."

This time Holden joined her. After they settled, he stole one final kiss, then patted her cheek.

"I guess I'm going to get back to it." Sabra returned to where they'd started her interview confessional. She snagged her camera then power-walked toward the stairs. She'd nearly escaped the field of raw sexuality surrounding him, which could be the only reason she'd do something so insane, when his warm fingers bracleted her wrist, drawing her to a stop against his solid chest.

"You can play it cool today. But tonight...tonight," he murmured against her temple, "I'm coming over to have pizza in bed. And *you* for dessert."

CHAPTER EIGHT

Holden figured these had been the best five weeks of his life.

Peaceful.

At the shop, he was surrounded by work he enjoyed and friends both old and new. Sex every night with a woman he counted as a partner more than a lover didn't hurt either. Watching her slave over her project, editing in the evenings, had showed him all over again how lucky he was to be part of the Hot Rods. Seeing his gang through her eyes as she discovered their quirks and documented their successes reminded him how fortunate he was. Doubly so now that he had her.

The sheer rightness of it all terrified him. Because he wished things could stay this amazing forever, and life seldom stood still for long.

If he were totally honest with himself, he'd admit they'd stalled somewhere safe. Afraid of hitting a speed bump early in their relationship, he'd kept things in low gear, retreating to Sabra's apartment every night.

They'd used feeding Sir Clawdius Fuzzington and access to her desktop computer, complete with post-production software, as convenient excuses to camp out at her place while avoiding the temptations and possible complications of spending their nights at Hot Rods. Soon, though, they'd have to cross that bridge and he hoped she was ready, because waiting to share her with the gang had started to make him antsy for more.

Maybe they could bring her cat over to Hot Rods. Fuzzi and Buster could turn out to be best buddies. Either that or mortal enemies. It'd be fun for everyone.

Holden leaned against a toolbox, crossed his legs at the ankles and stuffed his hands in the pockets of his coveralls. From the shadowed interior of the garage, he had a perfect view of Sabra's ass as she contorted herself into some ridiculous asana that left the other Hot Rod women gasping. In unison, they followed her directions for a simplified version of her expert yoga moves.

The women had taken to meeting up an hour before the shop opened to work out together. Nola swore the exercise helped with her morning sickness, though Holden figured the herbal tea Sabra had brewed for her had something to do with her settled stomach. Besides, no one around Hot Rods was going to complain if the ladies wanted to limber up. Get stronger than they already were.

During the day, things were business as usual. Swinger had knocked out some killer projects with Sabra hovering over his shoulder, prepared to show the world the quality and innovative style they lavished on each restomod completed at the shop.

Plus, Sabra spent an hour or two each afternoon conducting more interviews. Some with Tom and Ms. Brown were sure to tug at viewers' heartstrings and, hopefully, raise awareness for the shelter and adoption advocates across the globe.

As much as Holden hated to admit it, Sabra and Nola—okay, pretty much everyone except him—had been right. The show was a fantastic idea. Especially if it meant he got to hang around with Sabster all day, in addition to burning up the sheets with her at night.

"That's a view I'll never get tired of." Carver hopped up on the tool chest beside Holden.

"No kidding." Roman joined them. "I'm a fan of that really twisty one she does where she crosses her ankles behind her head then puts her arms around her thighs and behind her back. The guy who invented this shit was a genius."

"Yup. That's called the Sleeping Yogi pose and it's as good for fucking as you're imagining." Holden rubbed his chest as he remembered exactly how deep he could bury himself in Sabra's heat when she demonstrated that asana in private. "It makes her extra tight too."

"*Damnnnnnn.*" Alanso whistled softly when he peeked at the spectacle on the lawn. "If they would do that shit during the day, we'd have guys from two states away begging to pay double to get full service on their fill-ups."

"I prefer keeping them to ourselves." Bryce hummed as Kaelyn attempted an intermediate backbend. Long, flowing lines demonstrated the benefits of years of dance lessons.

They truly were lucky bastards.

Tom moseyed over from the main house and laughed at their impromptu huddle. "You kids are so predictable. Why aren't any of you out there practicing your moves?"

"'Cause it's much more fun to watch." Holden smirked.

"I didn't know yoga was a spectator sport." Tom snorted.

"Yeah, well, then you're not paying much attention." Kaige joined the fray. "Even Ms. Brown and Amber are getting in on the fun. You know, Ms. Brown is looking good out there. Pretty damn spry for an older lady. Maybe that cougar thing has some merit. I heard her ranting to Amber and Nola about finding herself a 'young buck' yesterday. What the hell did you do to piss her off so bad?"

Tom's head whipped around as he studied the impressive lotus pose Ms. Brown was folded into. With her eyes closed and her fingers curled as Sabra had instructed, she seemed like she could handle two men half her age. If she'd been venting to her daughters, Tom must really have screwed things up.

"Don't you kids worry about me." Tom groaned. "It's for the best that she moves on, doesn't get so attached."

"That's bullshit," Holden fired at his surrogate dad. They didn't pull punches around the garage. "If it was any of us falling for a woman, you'd tell us to plow forward, not turn tail."

"I think Swinger might have a point, Dad." Eli laid his hand on Tom's shoulder and squeezed. "It's obvious you have a crush on her. Do something about it."

"Who raised you jackasses to be a bunch of nosy busybodies?" With crossed arms, Tom refused to talk about it anymore despite his stare, which never left Ms. Brown as she stretched.

Holden forgot about giving Tom a hard time when Sabra got to the part of her workout where she unveiled the toughest of asanas. Inverted, she curled her legs while doing a handstand as easily if she were walking down a level, paved road. The scorpion. Next came the one that looked like she was kneeling on her upper arms, which tipped forward while she still maintained her handstand. The crow.

Witnessing her grace, poise and athleticism mesmerized him.

Without thinking, he trotted from the garage. Here was where she struggled. Every day, she came *so* close to the Two Leg Pose of the Sage Koundinya. She'd shown him pictures. To him it looked like she was supposed to curl into the fetal position on her side while supported by her arms beneath her knees. Damn near impossible.

But that didn't stop her from trying.

Relentlessly.

Focused, she didn't hear him approach. She slanted herself sideways as the rest of the Hot Rods women gawked, in awe of her skills.

At the crucial point, she wobbled. Her eyes scrunched closed as she prepared for impact with the ground.

Except, today, Holden lent her a hand. He put the barest bit of pressure on her wrists as she rotated. When she quivered, his brace kept her from crashing. As quickly as he'd assisted her, he removed his touch when she'd passed the split-second transition.

Sabra's eyes opened. She stared into his as she held the asana. Perfect positioning. Ideal posture. Nola's sister Amber whipped out her cell phone and captured the moment.

It must have looked as impressive on screen as it did to Holden's proud gaze because the women chirped and oohed over the shot.

After the requisite count, Sabra unfolded herself into the rest pose to cool down.

Today of all days, she needed the confidence. Later, she would present the Hot Rods pilot to the station execs. He wanted her to know he was with her.

Supporting her.

Her wide smile made it clear she understood. "Thank you, Holden."

Sabra leapt from the ground and tackled him. They rolled in the grass as he wrestled her beneath him. Laughter and kisses rained over them.

"Holden?" she whispered against his lips after a while.

"Yeah?" He didn't want to stop feasting on her, even if they were right in the middle of the Hot Rods lawn.

"I'm ready for more. Will you let me in? All the way?" A couple of worry lines appeared by her eyes as she bit the lip he'd so recently lashed with his tongue. "I trust you. And them. Together we can be more than we are individually. I don't want to be alone again. Never again."

"You won't be. Let's do this." He dropped lower, probably crushing her, but he couldn't help it. If he could have fused them completely he would have made them into one being. He felt like they might already be two halves of a whole. She was right.

It was time.

Tonight.

Or maybe a taste before her meeting. They'd planned for Tom and Ms. Brown to man the shop while they screened the pilot and gave her one final thumbs-up. They all knew it was a formality. They trusted her too.

"Guys, you ready to see your ugly faces on TV?" Holden rolled to his feet and stretched his hand out to Sabra, though clearly she didn't need his leverage to right herself. She took it anyway and made them both happy to be needed. And wanted.

Eli yelled to his dad, who'd cornered Ms. Brown over near the shed. It seemed like they might be having a heated discussion. "Dad, we're going upstairs. You have this? Or do you need one of us to stay?"

"Go!" Both Ms. Brown and Tom shouted in unison.

"That's not going to end well," Amber griped. She shook her head, then gave Nola a hug. "I'm off to work. See you all later. Take care of yourself and that baby."

She rubbed her sister's still-flat belly, patted Buster McHightops on the head, then waved to the gang as she left.

The herd of mechanics and their women funneled up the staircase to the apartment Sabra had avoided for the past month. He didn't believe it was because she'd thought stepping inside would give her cooties. Or put her in jeopardy—a la stranger danger, snatch-and-grab-style. At least he didn't think that was why she'd shied away.

More like she understood, as he did, this was a one-way street and once she drove down it, there'd be no going back to the simple, relatively normal relationship they had.

Temptation lured them and they'd fought it hard.

Now he couldn't remember why.

Fear ranked high on the list of reasons.

Unfounded.

Embracing the group and their unconventional ways only meant more affection for her, both to give and to receive. At some point he had to trust that she wouldn't abandon him. Neither would the Hot Rods. He sure as hell wouldn't dump Sabra to fend for herself as her parents had. Every one of them was better than the shit they'd sprouted from.

He laced their fingers as they climbed together toward their future.

Someone had already thrown a bag of popcorn in the microwave by the time they'd made it inside. Their appetites were legendary. Kaelyn needed to restock twice a week. The trunk on Bryce's Rebel AMC could barely hold their supplies. It was like feeding an army. Never did she complain. In fact, she seemed to enjoy kitchen duty.

Their skills and needs balanced out in a group this size. Someone provided for them all in one area or another. Sabra brought a lot to the table too.

Hopefully, nationwide exposure. An influx of business. Profits to pad their bank accounts and boost the shelter's capability to do good.

Suddenly twitchy, Sabra fingered the tiny drive that held so much of her hard work. And heart. She'd put all of herself into this program. More than the nightly news, the messages contained in the show seemed to matter to her.

Holden wasn't the only one who noticed.

"Don't chicken out now, Sabster." Carver smacked her ass. "Let's see what you've been up to behind that camera of yours."

The gang piled onto what had to be the largest sectional sofa in the northern hemisphere. They splayed in pairs or trios or whatever groupings pleased them. Many of their legs touched. Some people's heads rested in neighbors' laps. They were comfortable together. In every combination.

Sabra had a funny look on her face. He took a chance and whispered in her ear, "Jealous?"

"Kind of." She smiled and nodded.

One step at a time, he cautioned herself.

"Come on. Hand it over." Holden put out his palm and she dropped the flash drive into it. He inserted the memory into his laptop, then displayed the file on their Internet-ready TV. Before she could change her mind and stop him, the opening credits to *Hot Rods* blazed across the screen.

Nola had helped Sabra design them so that they were consistent with the shop's branding. Also, Kaige's fiancée had an amazing eye for graphics plus the skills to bring her ideas to life. Together, the ladies had created something that impressed him in the first few seconds.

The rest of the guys too, if their excited murmurs were any indication.

She'd incorporated black-and-white clips of each of them. The snippets said more to Holden about each man's personality than a photograph could ever capture. A smile from Bryce. Sally concentrating on an intricate design. Roman digging through the junkyard with Carver, quiet yet at ease with his roommate by his side.

She got them. Each of them separately and the mission of the shop overall.

The more he watched, the surer he was that she understood who they were individually and the unit they became when blended together. By the responses of the guys to her, letting her see inside their world, he knew they saw her as one of them.

Holden's cock grew harder with every frame that passed.

He watched his garagemates on screen as well as their expressions as they viewed the documentary Sabra had assembled. The bond was evident in their smiles, entwined hands and the downright naughty glances they shot each other.

By the time the episode had wrapped up, a sense of pride bubbled over in Holden. For all they'd built through hard work and love. The shop. For his misfit mechanic garagemates. And especially for Sabra, who'd seen straight to their core, despite scandalous relationships less open-minded people wouldn't be able to look past.

Dead silence rang in the room when the TV faded to black.

Sabra's foot jiggled a million miles a minute.

Before Holden could reassure her, Eli did it for them. As the head of the garage, it was his right. "You have my permission to show this to the execs. Or anyone else in the world. You're more talented than I realized, Sabra. This makes me love these fuckers even more, and I didn't think that was possible. The garage, these people, are everything to me. You captured all the qualities I appreciate about them and the work we do. Thank you for showing us that way. Helping the world understand who we are, even if they don't know what goes on behind the scenes."

Sabra hopped up from the couch, put one foot on the coffee table and launched herself at King Cobra, who caught her easily. He laughed as he hugged her in return and kissed the top of her head before lowering her gently to the floor.

"Watching that made me feel like we were worth saving." Roman didn't speak loudly, or often, but when he did, it was usually with a whopper that punched Holden in the gut. This time was no exception. "I can see it inspiring people to look harder at adoption. Thank you."

Eli beamed at Roman, then Holden. "I think your girl deserves a reward, don't you?"

Everyone in the room seemed to hold their breath. They looked around, at each other and finally to Sabra. Though her cheeks had flushed, she certainly wasn't running. Being the center of all that attention could have overwhelmed anyone, especially when seven men stared at you like you were being served up on a platter.

Which she sort of was.

Sabra returned to Holden's side though she didn't try to stop what was about to happen.

"We don't have a lot of time if she's going to get this over to the station so they can rave over the show." Holden stood up to make his proposal. "Welcome Sabra to our gang. Intimately. She's mine, and I plan to share her with you. Why don't we do something quick? Seal the deal. And later we can take our time. Get fancy. Celebrate together. Please."

He hoped he could introduce her to a whole host of possibilities later tonight. For a bisexual man, he hadn't had a guy in five weeks. Being here, now, when he was fired up was making him want things he wasn't sure Sabra had signed on for.

At least he could watch them fuck each other.

It was almost as good as them touching him while he made love to Sabra.

Almost.

Sally spoke up. "You don't have to beg, Holden. We've missed you. Did you have something specific in mind?"

She gave him the reins, knowing he understood best what would work for Sabra, and for himself.

"How about a game?" His grin probably had a wicked flare, but he couldn't bring himself to give a shit. Everyone knew he loved to play. Sabra practically purred as she rubbed up against him. He took that as a *hell yeah* from her.

"Which one?" Kaige wondered.

"Oral action. Guys on girls. Roman and Carver are a team. See who can make our partner come fastest. Winner gets to name their prize tonight." Holden planned to put his lithe tongue to good use.

Nola had already started stripping.

Holden peeked at Sabra. She glanced around the room with wide eyes, but didn't balk. Instead, she leaned into him when he walked her snug T-shirt up her flat belly, then over the mounds of her breasts. Her yoga pants draped over a lamp a few seconds later. Her body was gorgeous and toned, sleek as a cat's.

Several of the guys noticed and shared their appreciation.

Soon, everyone had joined them. They gathered into a circle around the coffee table. Some guys put their women on the couch and knelt between their legs. Holden decided to go full out. He lay on his back and urged Sabra to straddle his face.

"No head starts," Barracuda grumbled as he stripped Carver's jeans off.

The smell of Sabra alone was enough to have Holden aching. He reached around her slender thighs to unbutton his own pants and give his bulging cock some space. It flopped out and smacked his abdomen.

"I'm not waiting much longer. Everyone get ready." Holden nipped the inside of Sabra's thighs, returning her attention to him from where it winged around the room, taking in the passion his friends shared.

"You okay?" He kneaded her ass, holding her steady.

"Why did we put this off so long?" Her pussy already glistened with the proof of her arousal and he couldn't remember any of the seemingly valid reasons they'd stayed away either. Except now they came to the group as a couple instead of two people who'd just met. These past weeks had cemented their link and strengthened it. He hoped it could withstand the test they were about to put it to.

"Ready, set..." Sabra didn't waste another second. Holden chuckled as she gave the signal. When she screamed "Go!" it held a note of raw desire since Holden's lips curled over her clit and suckled.

He went for broke, adding his fingers to her clenching channel as soon as he was sure he wouldn't hurt her by stretching her tight passage. He shouldn't have worried. Her inner muscles sucked at him greedily, begging him to add another digit. Which he gladly did, though maybe not as deeply as he would have liked given his limited range of motion.

From this position, she had full views of everyone else and their devotion to ecstasy. Just as he had planned. And thankfully, she responded as if the pheromones flooding the room ratcheted her up instead of freaking her out or intimidating her. They were about to set a new record for this competition, he thought.

In fact, Holden probably would have won if Sabra hadn't distracted him, putting a hitch in his rhythm when he gasped. She bent backward, her spine arching until her ribs stood out on her lithe torso. The position put her mouth even with the head of his cock.

No way. She couldn't possibly…

She did.

Sabra sucked his cock as she ground her pussy on his face. A few seconds of that and he was a goner. Holden flicked her clit with the flat of his tongue and tried desperately not to choke on the arousal that flooded his mouth in response.

Both of them exploded simultaneously.

"Holy fuck, do you see that?" Carver groaned. "Damn, Swinger, your girlfriend is hot."

"Flexible too," Roman muttered reverently. "Now pay attention to your hand on my nuts and get your mouth back on my cock, boy. I want those lips to touch my belly. Take me as deep as you can. I'm going to come down your throat. And you'll thank me for it."

Sabra shrieked as her orgasm renewed. Did she get off on dirty talk, or was it the guys' play triggering her string of climaxes?

Holden fucking hoped it was the man-on-man action. After all, it ramped him up too.

Another blast of come threatened to overflow her mouth. Even when he thought he'd been drained dry, the combination of Sabra's sweet suckling and the rest of the gang around him could keep him coming.

Cries of completion echoed throughout the room as several of the Hot Rods licked, fucked and fingered their women across the finish line in rapid succession. Sabra perched on Holden's chest, petting his shoulders as she stared at the couples and the trio still working on their partners.

Maybe she had a bit of voyeur in her too.

She shuddered on top of him, her thighs clamping on his ribs with strong aftershocks or even possibly another mini-orgasm.

It seemed the women were treating their guys now, most of them getting off with a few sucks on their hyper-aroused cocks.

Rough breathing, low curses and proclamations of love drifted on the air.

Holden sat up, letting Sabra trail along his chest to straddle his lap instead. The moist heat of her pussy made his dick think of other fun and games they could engage in.

He hoped she didn't notice him getting hard again. Distraction time.

"Who won, anyway?" Holden grinned. As far as he was concerned, he'd hit the lotto with Sabra. Nothing else mattered except having her and being part of the gang. He took a second to smile down at her and revel in the joy that infected him when she grinned back.

"Nova," Alanso grumbled. "No fair. I think Nola's hormones are making her more sensitive."

"Don't be a sore loser, buddy." Kaige buffed Alanso's bald head. "It takes a hell of a lot more finesse to get her off without making the sensation too much these days. Not that I'm complaining. I'll be craving some rough stuff by the time she's ready to take me hard again, though."

Nola hummed and curled into her fiancé, looking as sleepy and contented as a kitten. "Me too."

They all chuckled.

Holden had an idea. Maybe he could convince Kaige to use his prize wisely. Tonight.

For now, he had one more trial run for Sabra. Could he push the limits just a tiny bit more? "Carver, did you get off from sucking Barracuda?"

"Nah. It's okay. I got what I wanted." He licked his lips.

Sabra surprised Holden by taking the words out of his mouth. "Would it be okay if I helped you out, Meep?"

Her gaze flickered from Holden to Carver. She'd shared a special bond with Meep from the beginning. Maybe because of the afternoon on the roof deck and maybe simply because they were a lot alike. Either way, Holden was glad she had someone else to confide in. Someone she felt intimate with.

Holden hugged her to him and kissed her with the hope he hadn't dared unleash these past several weeks. "Go ahead, sweetheart. Make him feel good. We'll do the same for you."

He had every intention of making it a positive experience.

Sabra crawled to where Carver sat on the couch and spread his legs apart. She knelt between them and reached out a tentative hand until she traced the length of his cock with a single fingertip.

Meep gasped, then reached for Roman's fingers as if begging for help staying still. The other man was happy to oblige, taking Carver's wrists in one hand and pinning them to the couch above his head.

"Can I suck him?" she asked Roman. The pair hadn't formalized their bond, but even Sabra could feel it. Holden beamed at her. He shuffled closer so he could rub her back as she pleasured his friend.

"Go ahead." Barracuda didn't smile. It seemed harder and harder for him to let Carver take what he needed. Holden hoped this wouldn't become a problem.

For now, no one thought beyond base primal instincts.

Sabra followed hers and kissed the head of Carver's cock.

The rest of the Hot Rods angled for a prime view, watching the induction of a new member. The respect and affection on their faces meant the world to Holden.

When he glanced back, Sabra had welcomed Meep between her lips and began to bob over his shaft. Though he had the smallest cock in the group, no one ever gave him shit about it because his orgasms beat all of theirs in intensity.

"That's right, Sabra." Roman ran a knuckle along her cheek. "He likes being in a nice, warm mouth. You know what else he likes?"

Carver whimpered as Sabra hummed around his cock.

Barracuda flashed a rare and predatory smile. He didn't expect her to let go of her treat long enough to answer.

"He loves having his prostate massaged." Roman used his free hand beneath Carver's knee to lift and bend Meep's leg so that his foot rested on the edge of the couch, opening him to Sabra's curious touch. Obeying Barracuda's silent command, Carver mimicked the pose with his other foot, leaving him completely exposed.

Sabra cried out around Meep's erection and her hips began to rock. Holden knew what she wanted. And he was glad to give it to her. Thankful she was on birth control, he knelt behind her and tapped her entrance with the head of his re-hardened cock.

"Teeth, teeth!" Carver yelped, making several people in their audience chuckle.

Roman smacked Meep's cheek, not too hard, and said, "Shush. You know you like a little pain with your pleasure. Say thank you instead of complaining."

"Thank you, Sabster." Carver groaned.

She chuckled around him, making another tortured sound escape from the man. It was all too much for Holden. He pressed forward and entered Sabra's drenched opening, beginning a slow steady fuck that he hoped he could maintain until she'd finished her gift to Carver.

Roman sank onto the floor so he could murmur instructions in her ear. Or maybe to palm her breasts. Probably both. He sucked her slender finger into his mouth, coating it with saliva, then said, "Go ahead and rub around his hole."

Sabra bucked beneath Holden, grinding onto his shaft. Swinger couldn't help but pump into her harder, faster. The tightening of her folds around him proved she loved any minute.

"Now put it in, a little at a time." Barracuda guided her hand.

"Curl your fingers, Sabra." Kaelyn added some of the wisdom she'd gained lately. The reminder of the Hot Rods presence resulted in Sabra's pussy clamping Holden's cock.

Oh God. It was better than he'd dreamed.

He fucked her harder. He wasn't going to last much longer. If she didn't come before him, he'd tag Roman to finish the job, though he'd wanted to wait until tonight, after she'd had time to process everything, to get to that stage.

Still, he wouldn't leave her wanting. That was never a danger with the gang of them nearby.

Roman put his hand between her legs, manipulating her clit. The added stimulation made her jerk. In a chain reaction, she must have hit Carver's prostate. He shuddered and cursed.

"There you go." Barracuda encouraged her to do it again and again. "Is his cock leaking yet? Yes? Good. Careful now, he'll come soon. Just keep going, right like that."

The escalation of Carver's bliss affected Sabra too. She mewled as she took pleasure from both him and Roman. Though she didn't stop the motion of her fingers, she allowed Meep's cock to slip from her lips when he begged, "Not yet, not yet. I want to enjoy it for a little longer."

Peeking over her shoulder, Sabra absorbed the impact of Holden's thrusts as well as the pure adoration in his regard. She watched as he fought the orgasm about to wash over him.

Dirty bastard that he was, Roman reached up and pinched Holden's nipple.

The sharp sting sealed his fate.

Carver must have liked seeing it too. He buried his fingers in Sabra's hair and guided her lips back to his cock. "Now, Sabster. Now. I want to come with him. You too. Let go."

Good thing Meep was primed. The moment Sabra's lips engulfed the head of his cock, he shot down her throat. She swallowed his fluids as Holden released into her again and again. Bookended by bliss, Sabra couldn't resist.

She rubbed her mound against Roman's hand, humping it so that her clit dragged over his fingers. It was all she needed to join the Hot Rods in a second wave of pleasure.

Guys cried out around her and women moaned. The pounding slap of flesh on flesh grew frenzied then slowed as others behind them found their own release.

Holden leaned forward, resting his head between her shoulder blades, pressing dozens of kisses to her neck. Several minutes passed in contented silence, until his softening cock slipped from her grasp.

They both moaned at the loss.

Carver ran his fingers through her hair, then patted her cheek. "Why don't you come sit up here? Cuddle. You'll be more comfortable."

Sabra winced. She glanced at her watch.

"I've got to get dressed. I'm almost out of time." Sabra gestured to her formal clothes for the proposal, then struggled to her feet. Carver steadied her.

Holden started to go with her, but wondered if he'd distracted her enough from her work. He should let her take some time to think about what had gone down and what lay ahead.

He knew it would be amazing.

Unable to resist the taste of Carver on her lips, he stood too.

After one final, lingering kiss, where they stared into each other's eyes—saying everything they needed to communicate with that look—he let her go, smacking her ass as she walked away.

***

Mind reeling, body humming, Sabra clutched her garment bag to her chest and hustled into the bathroom to freshen up and change. She glanced at her watch. Funny that she hadn't taken it off. She giggled to herself as she wondered what she'd looked like naked except for that.

Mentally, she calculated the time it would take her to get across town. Luckily, there shouldn't be much traffic at this hour. Hurrying would be to her benefit, though.

A soft knock came at the door. "It's me, Roman. Mind if I come in?"

What the hell? She'd sucked his lover's cock and come on his hand. What did it matter if he saw her getting dressed?

"Sure." She flipped the lock and admitted him, resisting the urge to cover her lacey bra with her hands.

"I can wait if you're not comfortable," he said.

"No, it's fine. Just habit, sorry." She shrugged and slipped into her blouse. As she fastened the buttons, she realized what he'd come into the bathroom for.

He snagged his toothbrush from the holder and went for the toothpaste.

Several times a day, he did the same thing in the garage's bathroom.

Sabra eyed her oversized purse. Feeling kind of sentimental after what they'd shared, she fished around until she came up with the package she'd stuffed in there a week or two ago after she'd noticed his habit. "I hope this isn't weird..."

"Nah. You get used to it. It's just sex, Sabra." He shrugged while meeting her gaze in the mirror. "If you're not okay with how this makes you feel, you should tell Holden now."

"What?" She shook her head. "I wasn't talking about that stuff. That's all good. Great, really."

A blush heated her cheeks.

"Then what did you mean?" Roman raised a brow, his toothbrush hanging from the corner of his mouth.

"I sort of noticed you have really good dental hygiene." *Lame.* But she couldn't think of a more polite way to say that it was obvious he was obsessed with it.

"Uh, yeah." He rubbed the back of his neck. Not one for talking, he didn't volunteer any info.

"So, I saw this at the store and I thought of you. It's a car. And a toothbrush." She held out the novelty to him. Meant for kids, it had called to her. Something about Roman's darkness hurt her heart and she wished she could help him smile, if only for a moment.

Holden's love for pranks and laughter made more sense to her by the hour she spent at Hot Rods.

"That's…" He paused and blinked at her a few times.

"Dumb. Sorry. I just thought—"

"No. It's awesome. I'm not used to people thinking about me, I guess. It surprised me." He rinsed his mouth out, then crossed to her. She held the gift out to him and waited for him to accept it.

With a crooked and scarred finger, he ripped open the blister pack, then spun the wheels on the cheap plastic brushmobile.

His smile warmed her better than a mug of cocoa on a frosty winter day.

And then he put his hand around the back of her neck and drew her to him for a deep, minty kiss. When he fed her his tongue, she shivered. Alpha and domineering, he touched her so differently than Holden, yet no less reverently. Fierceness and determination replaced the playfulness imbued in her boyfriend's liplocks. Barracuda compelled her to respond to his touch. She didn't resist.

"Well, guys, I don't think you have to worry about Sabster." Kaelyn cheered from the doorway. "She's making out with Roman in here like she's been a Hot Rod all her life."

Holden and Carver hooted from the living room. Swinger yelled, "I wanna see!"

Sabra and Roman broke apart, grinning at each other.

"Hey, I had to thank her properly for my present." He proudly displayed it to Kaelyn before depositing it in the cup on the edge of the sink then throwing his old, well-used one in the trash. "It's incredible. Thank you."

Then he ducked into the hall before shouting, "Don't you slackers have work to do? I'm going down to the shop."

When Sabra stepped into her skirt and reached behind her for the zipper, she realized Kaelyn still stood in the doorway. Her crystal-blue eyes were filled with tears.

"Oh my God. What did I do? Are you okay?" Sabra pinned her skirt to one hip and crossed to her friend. She hugged the woman with her free arm, though she had to reach way up to do it. Damn, she was tall.

"Wow. I'm great. That..." A pause stretched out as Kaelyn searched for the right thing to say. "You have no idea how special that was. Roman doesn't open up to just anyone. And especially about quirks like this. From his past."

"What? Oh, shit. Did I step in it?" Sabra winced.

"No, not if he's making out with you like that." The watery smile Kaelyn gave Sabra sent a blast of approval through her. "See, Roman brushes his teeth so much because his mom's rotted out. As a kid it terrified him thinking his would do that someday too. He didn't realize it was meth mouth. That it was a symptom of her addiction."

"Ah, fuck." Sabra felt her eyes bugging out.

"It's okay. You couldn't have known, and he seemed genuinely touched." Kae beamed. "Carver will love you forever for making Barracuda smile. It's not easy to do. Here, you want a hand with that?"

Kaelyn pressed Sabra's shoulder until she turned. In one quick motion she zipped the pencil skirt and tucked in Sabra's blouse. "Hang on a second."

The other woman vanished.

Sabra had barely finished packing her workout gear, fluffing her hair and putting some light gloss on her lips when Kaelyn reappeared. In her hands she held out a strand of pearls.

"You should wear these. They'll look beautiful on you. With that suit." Without waiting for an answer, she put them around Sabra's neck. "I don't have much from my old life, but I had these on the day I left home. I think that makes them good luck."

"Really? You'd lend them to me?" Sabra stared at the two of them in the mirror. The extent of her fortuity hit her like a semi. Not only had she gained the boyfriend of her dreams, but a whole host of readymade friends along with him. More than that even. After what they shared today, they'd become the sisters she'd never had but always wanted.

"Of course, you're a Hot Rod." Kaelyn squeezed her fingers. "You know, Tom says that we were all born Hot Rods, we just didn't know it yet. I like to think that's true. And I'm glad you've finally found your way home."

Pretty soon they were both reaching for the tissues.

"Sabra?" Holden called as he approached. "What's going on? You're awfully quiet in here."

She tried to erase the evidence of her crying but wasn't fast enough.

The sexy smile she'd come to adore melted from Holden's face. "You're upset? Oh, no. Sweetheart, come here. I'm sorry, I pushed you too fast. We can forget this happened. I didn't mean to rush you."

"Shh." Sabra covered his rambling with her fingers. "You're mixed up."

"Those are happy tears, Swinger," Kaelyn promised.

"Yep. Sure are," she confirmed. "And you'd better not take the Hot Rods away from me. Too late, buddy. There's no going back. Now that I know what I've been missing, I want to do that again. Soon."

This time it was Holden's lips on hers, telling her everything she needed to know with the skilled caress of his lips. When they had to breathe or pass out, he whispered, "Seriously?"

"Hell yes. Except not until I'm finished with my meeting. If you keep looking at me like that I'm going to end up being late. And that's not the way to impress the network execs." Her fingers trembled. So much rode on this pitch.

Together they walked down the hall into the living room where several of the guys lingered, about to return to work. Were they waiting to send her off with their blessings? It kind of felt that way. And she appreciated their support.

"Hey, I can't help it. Those smarty-pants you're wearing are pretty sexy." Holden winked at her as they rejoined the group.

"Swinger, you idiot." Rebel pointed to her bare legs. "She's got a skirt on."

"Well, it's a suit. That counts." Holden mimed panting. "I used to drool over those stuffy getups you wore on the news every night. Maybe later I can help you get undressed."

"You'd better count on it." Sabra laughed. She couldn't resist flinging her arms around Holden. He caught her to his chest and spun around a few times.

Today was definitely the best day of her life. And it was only going to get better from here.

"You're going to knock 'em dead, Sabster." Carver reminded her she had to get going.

"It's a big day for you. For the whole shop, really." Holden kissed her lightly then took her hand, heading for the door. "And if all goes well, I hope we can make it an even more important night."

"The Hot Rods do know how to party." Eli smiled as he hugged her, then angled her toward Alanso for his turn. They passed her around, offering words of encouragement and physical comfort. "Give us something to celebrate, Sabster."

"I'll do my best." Her smile threatened to rip her face in half as she made her way to her car and climbed inside. Pure elation left no room for nerves.

There would be plenty of time for that when she arrived at the station.

CHAPTER NINE

Sabra adjusted the jacket of her suit, pseudo-ironing a wrinkle with her fingertip. It felt odd to be dressed in her old uniform after the freedom to wear outfits more her style these past five weeks that she'd spent immersed in the Hot Rods garage. With Holden, who encouraged her inner spirit to shine through whether in her wardrobe, their lovemaking or any other aspects of her life.

She retrieved her briefcase from the car, then marched inside the station headquarters to meet with executives. Her pilot was solid. The show would be a smash hit. Convincing them shouldn't be difficult. As an intern, working her way up through the ranks, she'd sat in on any number of pitch sessions. Compared to the sketchy plans some people presented, her idea—complete with a detailed marketing plan—had them beat. Hands down.

Still, she couldn't shake the nagging sense of doom dogging her heels like Buster McHightops did when she had something yummy to eat. With a stretch of her neck first one way, then the other, she prepared herself for battle. If this didn't go right, her time with the Hot Rods would be at an end.

That thought had the potential to crush her. It hurt more than the idea of having to find yet another direction for her career.

As she strode through the doorway to her old world, Sabra was greeted by their friendly receptionist, Brenda. "Hey, lady, I sure miss seeing you around here."

"Same goes. How are your kids?" She leaned on the polished wood and got up to date. After that, Brenda's face clouded a bit.

"Sabra, I think you should know something before you go in there." She leaned closer and whispered conspiratorially, "Mr. Grills got promoted. Your old boss is in charge of programming and will be in on your pitch today. I overheard him bragging in the lunchroom that you didn't have a chance. He's pissed that you left. Not many people stand up to him. Don't take it too hard. It doesn't have anything to do with your proposal if they say no. It's him. You know how he can be sometimes."

Sabra couldn't catch her breath. She noticed the shudder Brenda gave and wondered if there was more to that story, but she didn't have time for any investigative reporting at the moment. Hell, she should pack it in and leave now, while she still possessed some scraps of her dignity.

The front desk phone rang. Brenda answered, then replied, "Yes, sir, she's here. I'll send her in."

And her window for escape closed.

Besides, she'd come this far and didn't plan on quitting now.

"Break a leg, honey." Brenda offered a weak smile, as if Sabra attempted to climb Mount Everest barefoot.

"Thanks." Keeping her chin up was tough, but she did it. Even when she saw Redford Grills camped out in the chair at the head of the boardroom table. Thank God Brenda had given her some warning. She owed the woman a case of their favorite cane sugar root beer.

"Grills," she said, her tone flat.

"Ms. Harp," he responded with a sneer.

"Good afternoon, everyone." She smiled brightly at the rest of the programming panel. People she'd known casually from the hallways at the station.

Several smiled as they welcomed her back. Grills' scowl erased their hospitality.

Sabra swallowed hard and drew on her yoga training to help her focus. She centered herself and concentrated on calming thoughts, like Holden's smile, for the span of a few deep breaths as she reached into her briefcase for a flash drive and a folder of handouts.

She passed the papers around the table, then plugged her memory stick into the projector as she had many times before while storyboarding feature pieces. "What I have for you today is a story about an amazing team of mechanics right here in Middletown. They're as philanthropic as they are adept with cars and have a modern edge that viewers will devour. There's something for everyone, from flashy cars to family values and a pretty big helping of sexy, tattooed men working without their shirts on."

A few people laughed, though not as many as she'd hoped.

"The briefing I've distributed contains facts about the episode plan, the benefit shelter and each of the co-owners of the shop, but I think you'll find that the pilot gives you the pertinent information in a much more enjoyable package."

At least they'd have the documentation to remind them of what they'd seen later. Nola had helped Sabra design the presentation and it looked pretty damn slick. They wouldn't forget her proposal anytime soon.

Without further hesitation, she clicked play on the pilot episode of *Hot Rods*.

She couldn't help her dreamy smile as Holden's slice of the opening credits rolled. Had she ever seen a man as gorgeous and wicked as him before? Hell no.

Tonight, they'd celebrate.

And after this morning's practice run, she knew she was ready for the real deal. No holds barred. Sharing with the group of Hot Rods. If they'd have her.

Time seemed to pass in a blink when she daydreamed about Holden. Or maybe Grills had terminated the viewing before the final scene?

Sabra squinted when he toggled the lights to full brightness.

"I think we've seen enough. Everyone's time is precious here, Ms. Harp." He emphasized that she had nothing better to do.

"I agree. Can I review the contract? I'll get back to you within the next twenty-four hours, as I know we need to air this pilot in the next few weeks to be considered for the national mid-season replacement." She expected him to brandish the necessary paperwork to secure the program, then send her on her way. Sure, he'd try to fuck her with unfavorable terms, but she had a lawyer ready to comb through the clauses and an agent who could negotiate on her behalf.

"Don't get ahead of yourself. As entertaining as that reel might have been, I'm not convinced of its mass appeal. Unfortunately, I don't believe we're going to be able to secure the amount of advertising necessary to support a docu-drama of this nature at our level, never mind rationalizing its widespread appeal to the national directors." Mr. Grills stared her down. "It's not racy enough to warrant a late-night spot and doesn't appeal to entire families."

"I beg to differ." Sabra sat forward in her chair, folding her hands on the table. "Do you know how many little boys would be entranced by the cars in the shop and the guys who build them? Their moms would be equally appreciative, I'm sure."

Grills laughed, though no one joined him. "Come on, Sabra. I thought you were smarter than to fall for this garbage."

"What does that mean?" She cocked her head. Her spine went as straight as if she had a metal rod for bone marrow.

"I'll be honest with you. Our sponsors aren't exactly pleased with you at the moment. The sudden change in the newscasting, without adequate transition, has tuned out loyal audiences." Grills stopped short of saying they'd liked *her*. "We've lost ratings. And advertisers haven't realized the returns they were promised. It's making them extremely hesitant to pledge for a show you produce. Even if you'd had a better quality idea, I couldn't sanction a risk like that for the station."

"What?" Sabra couldn't believe the crap he spouted. Even if it was true, it was his damn fault she'd left in the first place. Did no one else have the balls to stand up to this prick?

Given the slimy tactics he resorted to, she wouldn't be surprised to learn the footage he'd aired of Kaelyn and Bryce had been no accidental showing. He'd probably lied to her about slipping up. If he'd broadcast it on purpose to make trouble, he could have planned on taking the heat so she'd be beholden to him. The extent of his malice and power plays became clear to her. Sure, she had no proof, but her gut didn't lie. Her nose for news and her related bullshit meter lit up like a crazy Christmas display.

And suddenly she knew she never would work with the fucker again. Her ethics wouldn't allow it.

"Ladies and gentleman, I think we've seen enough—heard enough—to make our decision. Nothing here changes the concerns I raised to you in our pre-brief." Grills stood, and others followed his lead to maintain decorum. "Would you please excuse Ms. Harp and me so that we can finalize this sensitive discussion in private?"

Not a single person would meet Sabra's gaze as they filed from the room.

She'd never had a chance to succeed. Brenda had been right.

Damn Grills. She refused to let him take her down a second time.

If he didn't want this golden opportunity, she'd find someone who did.

"Sabra, I'm sorry." His tone changed in an instant as he locked the door behind the last corporate drone who'd evacuated the room. Something about the syrupy sweetness he'd never shown her before had the hair on the back of her neck standing up. "I realize these misfits are your pet project. You seem to have a soft spot for them, especially that Harold guy."

"His name is Holden." And hearing any form of it on Grill's disgusting lips made her want to retch.

"Ah, right." He chuckled. "Well, you see, we've done some research of our own on this gang. And it seems they'd be quite a liability. If anyone found out about their dirty secrets, including the picture we have of you sticking your tongue down Harold's throat and practically climbing him in public, they'd ruin the integrity of this family values baloney you're trying to spin. It was cute, a nice attempt, but…it ain't going to fly."

Sabra opened her mouth, then closed it again. How dare he criticize the Hot Rods' sexuality and act as if it had anything to do with their morality? She'd never met a group of people more loving, generous or decent in her life. This slimebag had no idea what he was ranting about.

"Unless…" He approached her, resting one flabby ass cheek on the table beside her, invading her personal space. "You were able to capture some footage of their affairs and incorporate it into the show. Now, *that* we could sell. Maybe even stir up some scandals ourselves to boost the ratings. If the Londons lost the precious shelter they claim to care so much about, maybe that could make for a whole second season."

"What?" She couldn't believe her show might have put the Hot Rods in danger again. "Are you crazy? No. No way. Don't you dare go near them or their foundation."

Grills held up his hands, palms out.

"I only have one other possible solution then, Ms. Harp." He scanned her from head to toe with an oily leer. "If you're so undiscriminating about whom you'll fuck these days, I suggest you put some of those wild child tendencies to good use. Show me how you blow your precious Harold and I'll consider changing my viewpoint. *I* won't even ask you to do my friends. And I'll offer you your old job back if you'll service me from time to time. A bargain, I think."

"Because your dick is so small I couldn't find it with a magnifying glass? Or because you'd shoot your tiny load in half a second if a real woman ever stooped low enough to touch your nasty cock?" She whipped around and stormed toward the door. "Fuck you! I would never betray the Hot Rods and I would double never demean myself in that kind of sordid arrangement. You know nothing about the Hot Rods if you think *they're* the immoral ones around here."

Before she could flip the lock, he'd caught up to her. His hand wrapped around her upper arm and squeezed hard enough to bruise. He yanked her toward the center of the room and flung her to the floor, where she knocked her skull on the base of a rolling chair.

The impact stunned her for a moment, long enough for him to hover over her and leer.

He probably thought he could easily take her by force in the soundproofed viewing room. But he didn't count on her training, or her willpower.

Sabra reached for her calm center and allowed him to sink lower. When he wrapped one hand in Kaelyn's necklace—choking her—and palmed her breast, she froze. A smirk crossed his face as he mistook her calculation for fear. Until he settled into striking distance. Then she elbowed him in the face while simultaneously bringing her knee up into his balls. She hoped she smooshed them like rotten grapes.

The resulting jerk of his body snapped the delicate strands around her neck, scattering precious pearls in every direction. It also secured her freedom as his hold on her evaporated.

Grills rolled and howled. She bolted, pausing only long enough to get in a solid whack with her briefcase to ensure he stayed down. She didn't stop when he bellowed her name or threats about libeling her to other networks. Nor did she pause when Brenda looked up from her desk with tears in her eyes.

Sabra ran to her car. She got in and drove. Drove until her mind went numb and she quit noticing the tears dripping off her face. She drove until her gas light came on and she thought she could face the gang without going ballistic. This riding out your anger thing had some merit.

Maybe she was a Hot Rod after all.

CHAPTER TEN

Holden checked his watch for the five thousandth time in twenty minutes. Sabra should have been back by now. It'd been hours. In the time it'd taken to have this one meeting they could have screened an entire season of a show, never mind talked about it. Hopefully that was a good sign, not a bad omen.

"Still nothing?" Sally came up behind him and rubbed his shoulders. The expert press of her fingers loosened the knots in his muscles, but they couldn't steal the dread in his gut.

"Not yet." He sighed.

Except, just then, the familiar purr of Sabra's car reached his ears. He turned to Mustang and hugged her quickly, then jogged out to meet his soul mate. Whoa. When had he started thinking of her like that?

Before he could freak out about the label change, she caused his thoughts to veer in another direction.

Sabra climbed from her car with her suit a wrinkled mess. Dark glasses hid her pretty eyes from his, though her splotchy skin made it pretty obvious that she'd spent at least some of the time they'd been apart crying.

He wanted to destroy whoever had hurt her.

"What the fuck happened?" Holden raced toward her, gathering her in his arms before she could answer. "Are you okay?"

Without answering, she snuggled into his embrace and soaked up his warmth. He rubbed her bare arms. She must have shed her jacket somewhere. Though the nights were growing colder as they headed for fall, the crisp air didn't warrant the shivers running through her.

Holden didn't press her to sate his curiosity. Instead he cradled her and gave her what she seemed to need. Someone to be there for her. He'd be that man whenever he could.

The guys noticed something was up and trickled out of the garage in their direction.

"Sabster!" Carver shouted, mistaking Holden's embrace for a congratulatory hug instead of a consolation. "So, how famous are we going to be?"

The shout woke her from her daze. She shoved away from Holden, teetering backward a few steps.

"Shh, easy." A croon passed his lips as he tried to get close to her again. She ducked her head and stayed out of reach. The woman in front of him bore no resemblance to the fighter he'd come to adore. Seeing her cowed and broken ripped his guts out.

Kaige and Bryce flanked her, giving her less room to run.

She froze, unintentionally trapped between the guys. Never before had she seemed frightened around them.

Alanso tipped his bald head toward Sabra's arm. "Yo, Swinger, what's up with that? Were the two of you rough with each other last night or do we need to kick someone's ass? I don't remember seeing that earlier."

His blood boiled when he zeroed in on the beginnings of a bruise, which stained Sabra's upper arm. He could make out finger marks. Like someone had grabbed her. A scan of the rest of her revealed another purple line around her neck.

"Who put their fucking hands on you?" He hadn't meant to ask her so harshly.

Still, she didn't flinch from his aggressiveness. Even after being manhandled so recently. Because she trusted him? He hoped so.

"It's not important." Sabra shrugged off his concern. Or tried to. The croak of her denial sounded nothing like her usual lyrical voice.

"The hell it isn't." Roman came to her defense. "Anyone who would hurt a woman, or a child, deserves to suffer."

The acid in his vehement stance was enough to trigger even Holden's nervousness. Enough of this insanity. Of this distance.

"Come here, sweetheart." He opened his arms and let her decide to accept his comfort or not. Thankfully, she did.

Sabra wrenched her sunglasses off, then flung herself against his chest. Horrified, he cradled her as her tears renewed. Her shoulders shook in his hands as she wept with noisy sobs. Without a clue, he looked to his friends, hoping for someone to make things better.

"Just hold her," Sally advised quietly. "Let her get it out."

Swinger lifted Sabra into his arms and carried her to the yard. He sat on the ground beneath a giant oak tree and cradled her in his lap as she bawled. If he hadn't seen it for himself he wouldn't have believed her capable of such an emotional display. At least not one this full of sadness.

Filling his hands with her was the only thing that kept him from balling them into fists, ready to pound whoever had done this to her. The Hot Rods gathered around, Nola offering Sabra some tissues when her crying dissolved into sniffles and then a couple hiccups. Then she looked to Kaelyn. "I'm s-sorry. Your necklace. It's gone."

"Nothing to apologize for," Kae said as she scooted closer to run her fingers through Sabra's hair. "I'm sure it wasn't your fault. I'm glad you came back to us. That's what we're here for."

Holden watched Bryce's girl snuggle into her man. Rebel held her tight. Despite her reassurance, it had to hurt losing her last link to her childhood home. Other than Bryce. And their Maserati, he supposed. It hadn't been very long since she'd fought her own demons and won. Hopefully they could help Sabra slay hers and move on to happier things. Please, let him be able to fix this for her. Or stand by her as she did it for herself.

"What happened?" Holden nudged her, his curiosity overwhelming.

"They rejected the show." Another sob accompanied her bad news.

"No. For real?" Eli looked as surprised as any of them. "Are they nuts? I wasn't sure at first, Sabra, I'm not going to lie. But the pilot rocked. I've seen the shit they put on TV. It's no contest."

"I think it's more to do with *me* than the concept." She closed her eyes. "Maybe I should talk to some of the guys at the station. Hand off the work to them. You shouldn't lose out because of me."

"No." Holden spit the refusal. "We work with you or no one. Why wouldn't they want you?"

"My old boss got promoted. Looks like he's in charge of programming now. He convinced the panel that the station's sponsors wouldn't back a show produced by me after losing money on their news advertising. I guess ratings are down since I walked."

"Of course they are. The only reason anyone watched the broadcast was to see you. Duh." Holden rolled his eyes, hoping to make her laugh. No go. Fuck.

"That might have boosted my pride after being out on my ass if it didn't mean that this project, which I care so much about, is a flop. Killed before it's off the ground. The message in *Hot Rods*—the value of the family you build—is so much more important than the crapstorm of negativity I reported on day after day. I can't give up. But there's no way…"

She trailed off.

"What aren't you telling us, *chica*?" Alanso peered at Sabra.

She bit her lip and shook her head. "Nothing."

"You seriously have got to be the world's worst liar, Sabster." Carver groaned. "You might as well spill. Holden's going to be worse than Buster with one of those ratty old sneakers he loves."

"Fine." She shoved out of Holden's grasp and climbed to her feet in a single graceful move. Pacing the lawn, heat began to replace defeat in her features. A major improvement. "They said they'd only consider the show if I made it juicier. They've heard the rumors around Middletown too. About you guys. They had pictures of me and Holden making out behind the pizza shop. They—"

"Get to the part where some asshole dared to touch you." Holden thought he could see where this might be going. "Your old boss? Is that who I need to bury in the basement?"

Sabra went pale. He reached out, but she evaded him, as if the thought of contact with him made her sick. Could she be afraid of him? He'd thought she knew him better than that, but that was before someone had hurt her, because of them. Him. He made a conscious effort to bury his rage.

"Let's just say he offered a Plan B that involved me on my knees." She looked away, her pretty smile nowhere to be seen, a flat line in place of her curved, luscious lips. Her fingers wandered to the darkening shadows on her throat. "I told him to fuck off, but he snagged me by Kae's necklace. If it hadn't given way…"

Sabra shuddered.

"Then I stand by what I said before." Kaelyn smiled softly. "It really was lucky, and I'm so glad you wore it today."

The women clasped hands.

Fuck control of his temper. If Kaige hadn't grabbed Holden in a bear hug, he might have torn out of the lot in a hurry. When he'd settled enough that the other guy let him loose, he huffed as if he'd run around the block a dozen times at full blast. Nova spoke into his ear, "Focus on her, not that jerkwad."

"Violence won't solve this." Tom must have heard the commotion and joined them, along with Ms. Brown. It figured he'd say that.

Holden hated that he had to hear the voice of reason. Pounding someone would have been so much more satisfying than this helplessness poisoning him. He concentrated on what he could do to make the situation better while Sally, Nola and Kaelyn rallied around Sabra, offering to go on a nut-cracking mission. Somehow she seemed to accept the feminine comfort more easily.

Holden did what Tom had taught him to do in times like these. He shifted away from emotion and engaged his logical side. "Can you rewind some? Before you almost made my head explode. And by you, I mean that fucking dickhead whose face I will likely rearrange sometime. Or at least dream about pummeling."

This time Sabra did giggle. It was weak, but she came through for him.

If she could laugh, they'd survive.

"Did you say they'd do the show if we gave them personal dirt?" He wondered if he could expose the most private parts of himself. The most important ones too. Where before he'd ruled it out, he considered it for Sabra.

"It doesn't matter. That was our bargain all along. No drama. No using the group's sexuality as a crutch. We don't need that. That isn't what the show is about." Sabra put her hands on her hips. "I'm not a sellout. And I won't let you be either."

Holden scanned the faces ringing him. Each of the Hot Rods nodded, except Kaelyn and Bryce, who couldn't participate in any of the filming because of the deal they'd signed with their families to buy their freedom.

"If this show is important to you, it's important to me. All of us. We'll do whatever it takes to make your dream a reality. Hell, I'll fuck you on live TV if that helps ratings." Holden shrugged then winked. "Besides, I think you'd get off on it. Showoff."

She wandered close enough to smack his arm. This time the tears in her eyes were mixed with humor.

"Thank you." Sabra did a slow spin so she could include everyone. "I mean that. The fact that you're willing to compromise your privacy. Subject yourself and the shelter to the criticism of ignorant people. Damn. I don't want to start crying again, but I know how much you prize that. I can't tell you what it means to me that you'd do that for me. So I hope you understand that I can't accept your offer. I would never do that to you. Any of you."

Holden started to speak, but she cut him off by stepping closer and wrapping her arms around his neck. She drew him to her for a light kiss then whispered, "Especially not you."

"Okay. Then what's the plan?" He didn't figure she'd quit.

The Sabra he knew would go down swinging.

"Maybe make some phone calls. There are other stations and markets to try. I'm not going to sugarcoat it, though. This was by far our best shot. You guys have some local notoriety. If I can't pull it off here, the odds aren't in our favor. Besides, I'm sure Grills has spread rumors about me to his buddies at other stations. He's well-known enough that people will ask him about me before investing. He can't risk my side of the story getting out. I know how he works. He'll have covered his ass by telling his buddies to look out for me. I can't imagine them signing the show. Hell, I don't think I'll even stand a chance at pitching the pilot. They're going to write me off before I can get a foot in the door." She sighed. The bleakness in her eyes as she lowered from her tiptoes and unwound herself from him caused his chest to ache. "Maybe I could crowd source private funding for production and online distribution, but that kind of project—even if it finds a cult following—won't have the immediate impact of broadcasting on a major network. Everyone knows one of these local pilots is getting picked up for the mid-season replacement on the national level. I know this show has the potential. If they saw what I saw it would be a done deal. I'm sorry. I feel like I've let you down."

Several of the Hot Rods grumbled at that. Sabra didn't seem to notice, her stare planted firmly on the grass.

"I'm going home to feed Sir Clawdius Fuzzington, then I'll see if I can brainstorm a solution." Her shoulders sank the more she talked.

"Let me grab my jacket." Holden jingled his car keys in his pocket.

"I don't think I'll be good company tonight. You should stay here, where you belong." The crack in her voice nearly broke his heart. He didn't care to pile tension between them onto the disastrous day she'd already had. If she used the night alone to lick her wounds, she'd come battling back stronger in the morning. At least he expected her to.

"Let me drive you. You're upset..." He reached for her hand but she shrank away.

"I'm better now. Just kind of...empty." Sabra stood straighter. "Thank you, but I'll be okay. I'll text you when I get home so you don't worry, okay?"

Not really. But he didn't have much choice.

"I'm just a call away. Any time of the day or night. Change your mind and I'll be there in a few minutes. You know that, right?" Holden tucked a strand of hair behind her ear.

She nodded and surrendered a stealthy sniffle. At least it wasn't more of those sobs that threatened to shred his soul.

The urge to say the three words he'd been choking on a lot lately burned strong. Still, he bit back the promise, sure this wasn't the right time to tell her how he felt. Freaking her out more wasn't part of his plan.

Sabra hugged him tight yet far too briefly.

And then she was gone, walking toward the parking lot with her shoulders back and her head up. Stubbornness alone put the steel in her spine. He loved her more for it.

Tom rested his hand on Holden's arm, as if he might run after her.

Gears spun in his mind. What could he to do give Sabra this?

Hot Rods stuck together, and whether she knew it yet or not, he was sure down to his bones that she belonged with them. But what did he know about her world?

Networks, programming, sponsors...

Well, shit. They had plenty of vendors who would piss their pants to reach an audience across the county with interest in old cars. Fixing up classics required plenty of their products. Excited, Holden decided to see if he had the gist of it right.

"Nola." He turned toward the rest of the gang. Kaige sat on an old tire they'd hung parallel to the ground. He held his girlfriend in his lap and rocked her and their unborn child gently. The guy rubbed her back, keeping her as calm as possible despite the cloud of gloom hanging over the whole garage. They'd each come to care for Sabra. That meant something to Holden too. If they worked together…

"Nola," he shouted again as he approached.

Nova shot him a warning glance that Holden ignored.

She lifted her head off Kaige's shoulder and looked up to Swinger with big, glassy eyes. Before she could speak, he jumped right in. "Those vindictive fuckbuckets rejected the pilot because of a supposed lack of advertising interest, right?"

Nova's dreads shifted around his head as he nodded in tune with his girlfriend.

"Well, then what if we were to show them they're wrong? That it's worth their while and then some. Do you think they'd back the program if I could assemble a list of vendors who'd promise cash if they put her in the national spot? We know a ton of people. Have great relationships with our suppliers. Kaelyn has them wrapped around her finger now that she's handling the ordering. Plus, a ton of them are startups that one or all of us have known for years." He tried not to get ahead of himself, but his hands flashed out as he gestured to emphasize his hypothesis. "Would that work, you think? Could we raise pledges tonight before they announce the replacement show for the hole in the Fall lineup?"

"I'm sure we could." Nola winced. "But, Holden, do you know how much money we're talking about? I'm guessing it's millions."

His heart deflated as hope leaked from it like a wilting balloon.

"Are you kidding? That much?" He rubbed his temples.

Bryce did some mental math, ticking things off on his fingers. "I think it's doable. Nationwide coverage. An enormous audience. If we could get two hundred people to pledge ten grand each, that would get us in the ballpark. At least enough to show real potential."

Holden gulped. It wasn't going to be easy.

"Then I guess we shouldn't waste any more time chitchatting." He took a deep breath and prepared to burn up the battery on his phone.

Tom edged closer and clapped Holden on the shoulder. He fully expected to hear another speech about impulsive behavior and wishing things into reality. Instead, the only father he'd ever known squeezed him in a one-armed hug. "I like they way you're thinking, kid. About this whole thing. Sabra included."

"Really?" A sliver of hope crept into his heart. And if they could pull this off, maybe she would see she wasn't an outsider anymore. As surely as her parents had adopted her, the Hot Rods had staked a claim too. She could be one of them if she wanted to be. Maybe the two of them could move forward, as an integrated part of the group.

Ms. Brown took up a place on his other side. She didn't settle for a man hug, though. Her arms wound around him and squeezed surprisingly tightly. "You really care for her, don't you?"

He didn't figure he had to answer but he nodded anyway.

"Sabster *is* pretty cool," Carver added.

"Hard to imagine what she sees in a jokester like you, but we won't let you lose her, Swinger." Roman broke his usual silence to add reassurance.

Did they feel it too? A sense of doom. If this fell through, Sabra wouldn't be there anymore, with her camera shoved in everyone's business, and not tied to them after hours either. She might have to move to find a better opportunity for her career if the local network kept cockblocking her.

Unacceptable.

He wanted her to be part of their family. Permanently.

Eli took charge, slamming full-force into boss mode. "Kaelyn, will you divvy up the vendor files? Sort that fancy spreadsheet you made with details on who we do business with. Start with the ones we shell out the most to in an average year. Each of us will take the companies we know best. Sally's got her paint suppliers. Holden, you take the lead with the leather manufactures. Alanso, what about that new engine outfit? Tell them we'll feature their products—guaranteed air time, when we have appropriate projects—in addition to the standard commercial advertising."

"I'll check with Amber." Ms. Brown referred to Nola's sister, who ran an event planning business along with Kaelyn. "Maybe some of her current clients, or the ones from her consulting days, have interest in this special publicity opportunity."

"I'll call a board meeting at the shelter," Tom pitched in too. "They'll be glad to contribute when they hear about Sabra's angle on this thing."

"First one to twenty sponsors gets—" Bryce cut off before he got to the naughty part when he remembered Tom and Ms. Nola were there. He finished lamely, "—a nice surprise."

Holden couldn't help but laugh. He scratched his chin. "You know, I think we might be able to get this done."

"So quit standing there and let's get to work." Eli ruffled Holden's hair, then took off for the garage. Each of them followed. Together.

***

Five hours later, they had to call it quits. They'd already woken up a few people on the East Coast, which didn't make them all that receptive to the Hot Rods' proposal, and had exhausted the list of West Coast vendors. Kaelyn crunched the numbers from the slips they'd handed her after each conversation as they huddled around her in the garage office.

"I'm sorry, Swinger." She looked at him with gorgeous blue eyes that couldn't disguise her sadness. "We're still two-hundred thousand dollars short of the goal. And that includes a large contribution from Hot Rods. Nola says we can't justify more than that out of our advertising budget."

His shoulders slumped. They'd gotten so close. Hell, he'd kick in the rest himself if he had it, but he'd already poured in his life savings under a phony vendor name.

"Think!" he roared at himself.

A few of his friends flinched. It wasn't often he raised his voice.

Buster McHightops whined and flopped into the corner, resting his head on his paws. Even the puppy was exhausted.

"Hang on. It's a long shot, but let me try something." Cobra lifted the receiver of the office phone and set it on the desk. He hit the speaker button.

Everyone held their breath as he punched one of their speed dial buttons.

Holden's heart hammered. Why hadn't he thought of this? It might not be worth it for them but...maybe...

On the second ring, Mike, the foreman of the Powertools crew, answered their call for help. "Isn't it late for you to be hanging around the office?"

"Hey, Mike, it's Eli. We're still working for a reason. I've got the rest of the gang here too. You're on speaker phone."

"Figures. Since you guys do everything together these days." The guy laughed. "And you know I'm a fan of that. Hang on, we're actually enjoying the deck at Kayla and Dave's house. Let me put you on speaker too. It'll be fun."

"Unfortunately, this isn't a social call." Cobra cleared his throat. The guy hated asking for help with anything. Swallowing his ego, he did it anyway.

That he would for Sabra, for Holden, meant the world.

"What's up?" Murmuring in the background made it clear the rest of the crew and their wives were listening in.

"You know how you always tell us we have a favor to call in with you guys?" His mouth pulled into a grim slash.

"Yeah, of course," Dave responded before anyone else could.

"We could use a hand. And by hand, I mean cash." Eli gritted his teeth.

"I thought the business was doing great?" Joe, Eli's cousin, asked.

"It is," Holden jumped in. "The money isn't for the shop. It's for Sabra."

"Oh." One of the crew wives gasped. "Is she okay?"

"Yes, sorry. Didn't mean to scare you." He said, "The station won't give her pilot a shot because her piece-of-shit ex-boss is fucking with her, drying up the funding by spreading rumors about her being unreliable. If she doesn't get on there, she doesn't have a shot at the national slot. It's a bullshit tactic, but it's working. We've been pounding the pavement all night, drumming up investors worthy of a national program, never mind screwing around at the local level. We think we've got almost enough for them to take her serious but..."

"How short are you?" Mike asked. "And are you talking about a donation? Or an advertising buy?"

"You'd get sponsorship. I'm not sure exactly how that could work for you guys..." Holden sighed.

Neil jumped into the discussion. "We build a hell of a lot of garages, dude. Guys with discretionary income, who want something beyond the ordinary to house their collections make really fucking great customers. We could put together a commercial featuring some of those high-end jobs we've done. It's a good business. Profitable. Plus, we know tool suppliers who could cross-promote on a show about cars, don't we?"

A flurry of agreement came from the other end of the phone line. Holden's stomach did cartwheels as he listened to their enthusiasm growing.

Morgan spoke up. As a business owner herself, she helped the crew with their finances and budgeting. "We could drop a hundred thousand for the right deal."

Dead silence from the Hot Rods.

"It's not enough, is it?" Mike asked.

"Half of what we need," Holden confirmed. "Look, we won't take any more than that from you. It's beyond generous."

"Shit," one of the guys cursed.

Then Devon piped up from the crew side. "We can promise you half right now. I'm sure we can find the rest from people we know in the morning. Put us down for two hundred thou. We'll cover it by selling half of our share."

"Are you sure?" Eli gripped the edge of the desk as he looked around the room. Each of the guys and their women seemed to hold their breath as the crew murmured between themselves until they reached agreement.

A few heartbeats later, Mike's clear, authoritative answer sealed the deal. "Yes. Definitely. Do it."

The Hot Rods roared, a few people landing thumps on Holden's back.

He didn't hear any of it. Didn't feel a thing. Couldn't see or breathe. The only thing he could imagine was the look on Sabra's face when he broke the good news to her first thing in the morning.

Holden wished he could be there to hear her tell her ex-boss to shove his sabotage attempt up his wrinkly, old ass. And hopefully slap a sexual harassment suit on his desk to boot.

CHAPTER ELEVEN

Sabra rolled into the Hot Rods lot with sickness coating her guts. It felt like she'd swallowed a handful of the river rocks she'd decorated her yoga studio with. After an entire night of meditation, she had no clue how to proceed with her life. Nothing met the requirements for a satisfactory solution. Either she had to give up Holden and look for a job elsewhere, beyond Grill's reach, or she had to be a bum.

Opening a yoga studio of her own was the best Plan B—or was it Plan F by now?—she could think of. Resistant, though, she hated turning the one thing that relaxed her into a business. Plus, then the important social messages she advocated would remain unheard.

Part of her knew she'd be unhappy settling for something less than her best, even if it meant she got to keep the man of her dreams and the friends that came with him.

Without him, success wouldn't be enough to keep her happy.

She was officially screwed.

Buster McHightops barked and ran over to greet her with happy puppy licks completely at odds with her frazzled mental state. Irresistible, he lured her into petting him, then slurped a lined across her cheek when she knelt.

A laugh escaped the tightness strangling her.

"That's the sound I love so much." Holden strolled from the garage. He didn't wag his tail like Buster, but she knew he'd been waiting for her. Banishing him from her apartment last night, refusing to stay with him, had been tough, but she'd better get used to it.

She smiled sadly at him, kind of surprised by the answering grin he flashed her.

Didn't he realize things were in the crapper after yesterday?

Cheering his friends came naturally, but he'd have his work cut out for him today. Nothing could lift the murk that had descended on her heart.

Unless it was what he said next.

Holden put out his hands and drew her to her feet when she laid her fingers in his. He tugged her to him and administered a bear hug the likes of which she'd never received before. When she looked up at him with questioning eyes, he covered her mouth with his.

Enveloped in his heat and protection, it'd be easy to believe things would be okay.

Except they weren't. Wouldn't be.

"I want to tell you how much your pilot of *Hot Rods* impressed me." He refused to let her interrupt, so she listened. Really listened to what was so important to him. "When I saw us through your eyes, I could feel how much you loved the Hot Rods. And I want you to know I feel the same. About you. Us."

Silent tears made tracks down her cheeks. Damn him, she was tired of crying.

He paused to kiss them, then continued, "Every one of us here believes in you, your work and your place in our gang. That's why they spent all night raising sponsorship money. We've secured two million dollars of pledged advertising spend for commercials run during *Hot Rods.* So you can tell your old boss to take that and stuff it where the sun doesn't shine. Then buy your show."

"What?" Thank God he was holding on to her or she would have flopped to the ground in an apoplectic fit.

"Yep. Two mil. Guaranteed. Only for you and your program." Holden's smile nearly blinded her.

"You did that, for me?" She swallowed hard, terrified and more queasy than before. "Please tell me you didn't call in any big favors or anything."

"Uh, okay. I won't say that." He lost some of his easy looseness as he studied her face. "Sabra, what's wrong? I kind of thought you'd be jumping my bones about now. What am I missing?"

Shudders racked her and her teeth clicked together.

"I can't accept that." She groaned.

"Sure you can. Everyone who signed on stands to benefit too. They're not doing it to be generous. The show is going to be a hit and they want to ride the wave. Sell their products." Holden frowned. "What's really going on here?"

"I might not have told you the full extent of my run-in with Grills yesterday." She clenched her teeth, angrier than ever that some son of a bitch had the power to ruin her life.

"Did he hurt you more than you let on?" Holden's hands ran over every inch of her he could see as if x-raying her with his fingertips.

"I'm okay. But I won't work with him." She couldn't put herself in that position. "And even if I file a lawsuit against him, which I am considering if only to help other people that may be abused by him, it won't be speedy. Plus, there will be all kinds of residual issues."

"Damn, Sabra." Holden rocked her against his chest. "I wish you'd told me yesterday how badly he scared you. Or what he did. The guys wouldn't *really* let me kill him, you know. They don't want me in jail. But I sure as hell would make sure you're safe. Always."

"I have no idea what's going to happen now." She squelched the tears that loomed near the surface again. Crying was not her thing. "But, Holden, I love you too. I can't believe you did this for me."

"We'll make it work. Somehow." He rested his chin on the crown of her head and held her tight. "What you did was special. The world deserves to see it. I think it could make a difference for some kids out there. Kids like us."

Slipping her hands into the back pockets of his jeans, she held on tight and prayed he was right. It'd been stupid to leave him last night. Surrounded by his strength, she found hope again. Even if it was foolish.

They stood there for a long time.

Until someone burst from the garage shouting their names. Eli. "You guys didn't talk to the station yet, did you?"

Holden separated them only enough to make eye contact with the head of their gang. "No. We've got a situation."

"With the show?"

"No, with her ex-boss. She won't be working with that creeper. Now or ever. There's no way she's selling to the station." Holden didn't question her. He trusted her instincts and had her back. Even if it meant going against his friends until they could understand his objections.

Eli looked first at Swinger and then Sabra. He nodded. "I want to know the details later. But for now, don't say that too loud. I just got a call. From Mike."

"He's the foreman of the Powertools crew?" Sabra double-checked. They had a *lot* of friends.

"Yeah." Eli replied. "They wanted to let us know they came through on the extra hundred grand in sub-pledges. *Plus* it turns out one of the guys they called, Denver Hart, is interested in placing a competitive bid. He's an exec at one of the independent cable networks. Turns out the crew built a fancy-ass garage for the dude to house his collection of Lambos. Well, a leading actor in one of his series wrecked his bike. The guy didn't make it and they can't do the show without him. They're in a bind and they need something to put in its place quick. *Hot Rods* appeals to the same demographic. He wants to see it."

Sabra couldn't speak. Her mind went blank and stars danced across her vision.

"Yo, Sabster." Eli snapped his fingers in her face. "Don't check out over there. This is good news. Right?"

"Right?" Holden echoed.

And this time she couldn't hold back the tears. Happy ones. "Yes. It's a miracle."

"Okay, well, get your shit together. You two are going on a road trip. He wants to meet you in person and he wants a screening of the pilot before he can vouch for you to his executive team. So you have to get your asses in gear." Eli handed Holden his keys before smiling at Sabra. "See you when you're the producer of this year's hottest show. Swinger, drive safe. And fast."

Before anything could happen to change the man's mind, Sabra grabbed Holden's hand and sprinted toward his sexy car. After a few steps she did a one-eighty and ran back, throwing herself at Cobra. She smothered him in hugs and kisses before dropping to the ground and tearing off toward a laughing Holden once again.

"You're welcome!" Eli shouted through cupped hands around his mouth. "Kill it!"

The ride there was tense and quiet as Sabra practiced her pitch in her mind and Holden concentrated on delivering her to the appointment in record time. The meeting passed in a blur that resembled a dream. The independent network could take chances. She could add more commentary, have full creative control and make buckets of money. By the time they'd left the building, she had a handshake agreement and a future brighter than she'd ever imagined possible unfolding before her. The pilot had an airdate. Depending on ratings, they could have a deal.

When she emerged and caught sight of Holden, leaning against his car with his ankles crossed, she nearly dropped dead from an overdose of lust mixed with love. *Love.*

They'd said it.

And meant it.

Now she couldn't wait to share the sentiment with the Hot Rods. Emotional and physical connections. If they hurried, they could make it home tonight.

Sabra launched herself into his arms for a congratulatory make-out session. Before they ripped each other's clothes off right there, she twisted out of his hold, then hopped through the open passenger window of his Swinger as if she were a stunt double for one of the brothers on *The Dukes of Hazzard*. If she flashed him in the process, all the better.

"That's fucking sexy," Holden growled as he took his place behind the wheel. Proving that great minds thought alike, he said, "We can be home in four hours. I think it's time we celebrate properly."

"By properly, do you mean you're going to watch your friends fuck me?" She shifted so her back pressed into the door and her legs spread wide. Rubbing herself drew his attention from the road and they swerved. Okay, better hold off on that.

They both laughed.

"If I don't manage to kill us before then. Hell yes." He moaned. "I'm so hard right now I could use my cock as the gear shifter."

"Can I ask you something?" She schooled her features to stay calm and open, unthreatening. Never would she judge him.

"Of course." Holden answered automatically.

"Before you were with me, did you ever get it on with the other guys? Like Eli and Alanso, or Carver and Roman or whoever else?" Sabra had sure as hell pictured it since Roman had casually touched Holden during their group encounter.

"Ah, shit. Does it matter?" He swallowed hard enough to make his tan throat flex.

"Only if you're not doing it now because you think you can't." She smiled at him. "I want you to have everything you need when you're with me. And if that includes being with them, then you should do it."

"Seriously?" He shot her a glance from the corner of his eye.

"As long as I can watch. Yeah. Definitely." Sabra squirmed in her seat, wishing they were closer to home.

"You're killing me, Sabster." A groan rumbled from his chest. "We might have to make a pit stop at the next rest area."

"Yep. Yep, we might." She whipped out her phone to look for the closest one along their route.

"But then again, that will make it take longer to get home. And there are things I'm dying to do when we get there." He passed a car fast enough to make it look like the other vehicle was standing still instead of flying down the highway at the speed limit.

"So after you watch me, I get a turn, right? I want one of the guys to fuck you while you screw their girl. Will you let me see that, Holden?" Bravery flooded her, secure in his unflinching love and the lengths he'd go to for her happiness. She owed him the same.

"You'd want to see me bottom for a guy?" He tried to be casual, but the careful stillness in the way he held himself gave him away.

"Are you afraid of losing me if you say you need that?" she asked him point blank.

He glanced over at her, then back to the road. "Yes."

"You don't have to be scared, Holden." She slid over so she could rest her palm on his thigh. "I love you, remember? All of you. Whatever you need, that's what we'll do. And I'll love every moment that I get to witness your pleasure. Your happiness makes me happy."

"I would like that, then. Except…" He paused.

"Yes?" It was important to her that he get exactly what he wanted.

"What if I was fucking you while one of the guys did me? I want to be a part of both you and them at the same time." He gripped the wheel and licked his lips. "If you want to watch another time, that's totally cool, but tonight—I want to be with you."

"That's…" A wave of lust blinded her temporarily. Imagining it was easier now that she'd seen them all take their pleasure. It blew her away.

"It's okay if it's not your thing," he hedged.

"It's *so* my thing." After placing a kiss on her palm, she reached across the car and touched his cheek. "*You're* my thing."

"I really do love you, Sabra." He shifted into sixth gear and flew along the highway toward home. "And I can't wait to show you how much. Tonight and always. If you feel differently when it's actually happening, that's fine too. You can tell me. You say stop and we do. For tonight or longer. Until you're ready, or forever if that's what makes us happy."

"Stop worrying." She slid her hand higher until she cupped his hard cock. "I've been thinking about it for weeks. What it would look like, sound like. Twice as often since the send off you guys gave me yesterday morning. Pure hotness is all I can imagine. I want this. I'm dying for it."

Holden cursed when red and blue lights flashed in the rearview mirror, accompanied by a siren. "Shit. Well, there went that extra time we made up."

"Probably I shouldn't tell him why we're in a hurry, right?" A coquettish smile graced her lips.

Holden was still laughing when he rolled down the window to talk to the officer.

***

Sabra held Holden's hand as they entered Hot Rods. Suddenly nervous, she wasn't sure what waited for them inside. After they'd gotten their ticket, they'd slowed the pace a bit and the longer drive home seemed endless to her, though the time-out had given him a chance to text the Hot Rods before they got going again.

At least she assumed he had when he opened the door and revealed the whole lot of them lounging naked beneath a cloud of balloons and a banner that read, *Congratulations, Sabster.*

The lump in her throat bulged when she spied another one that read, *Welcome home.*

Somehow, she figured they realized how entangled their futures had become. Not only were they accepting of her presence in the garage and in their group, but they were also excited about it.

Who was she to turn away?

Sabra pounced on Holden's back. He instinctively grabbed her legs and whooped as he ran to the living room and deposited her in the middle of the Hot Rods, both of them laughing like fools in love. Because they were.

She searched her heart for the right thing to say as she scanned the room and the people surrounding them with shared joy. In the end, talking was unnecessary.

Before she could utter a word, Kaige stepped forward. He looked back at Nola and she nodded once, definitively. "I've decided what I want as my prize from yesterday's game."

Sabra shivered when he encroached on her personal space. He leveled a sexy gaze at her that singed her with heat he'd never blasted full-on in her direction before. She squeaked, "Me?"

"Damn straight, Sabster." He didn't hesitate, his hands flashing forward to grab her blouse and rip it apart, buttons popping. As the plastic bounced on the concrete flooring outside the area run, he stroked his rapidly hardening cock. "Don't act like you don't want me to fuck you. Like you don't want Swinger to watch."

Her mouth went dry. Not from fear. From white-hot desire. And anticipation.

"Is this still what you want?" Holden whispered in her ear from behind her, where he braced her with his hands around her waist. His hard cock nestled in the valley of her ass told her everything she needed to know.

"Yes." She stared unblinking into Kaige's eyes as she answered. "If it's okay with Nola."

"I wouldn't be here if it wasn't." He winked at her before resuming his steamy advance. "I wasn't lying yesterday when I said she's grown sensitive lately. I would never hurt her. But you can give me what I'm craving. Swinger can give you to me."

In fact, he reached around in front of her and unfastened her skirt, then lowered it to the floor. Mindlessly, Sabra stepped out of the fabric, then kicked it into a corner somewhere.

She shrieked when Holden lifted her off the ground and held her out toward his friend. An offering. Sabra didn't hesitate. She kept her legs straight, raised them and grabbed her ankles, then spread them, giving Kaige a pretty clear picture of how she saw this playing out.

"Fuck," he growled, and his nostrils flared. "You're like a sex goddess with this yoga stuff."

"I never realized it would have so many benefits." She giggled, making Holden do the same behind her.

Kaige paused, his fingers a fraction of an inch away from her pussy with all the Hot Rods looking on with rapt attention. Crossing that tiny gap meant a change for every one of them.

When she didn't object, and neither did Holden, Nova did it.

He tested the wetness of her pussy and the fit of her snug sheath around his fingers.

"Damn." He groaned. "I was going to go down on you, but I don't think you need me to, and I'm dying to fuck you. Have been for weeks. If I could spank you, I would right now for teasing us every day."

"Another plus for exercise." She beamed.

Kaige asked Holden, "Do you want me to wear a condom with her?"

"They're clean, Sabra. It's your call. I know you use the patch." He kissed her neck. "I'd love to watch their come dripping from you right before I stick my cock in your pussy."

"Yes." She could only manage one word.

Kaige aligned their bodies, then sank inside without further delay. Joining with him felt different, yet right. With Holden cradling her, she soaked in the new sensations.

In the background, Nola cried out. Sabra tensed, wondering why, but when she realized that Roman and Carver had flanked the other woman and were giving her pleasure of her own. Gently. Sabra relaxed.

Nova plunged deeper, then retreated a bit before plowing inside her again.

Holden stared down her torso to study the intersection of their bodies. "God, you look amazing. So hot. Sexy. I can't believe you're mine."

"You did good, Swinger." Kaige grinned. "Now hold her tight and lean into my thrusts. I need to fuck."

Sabra let her head fall back onto Holden's shoulder as he held her up and open for his friend to pummel. The force of Kaige's strokes rubbed her in all the right places, especially when his pelvic bone tapped her clit with every plunge.

A particularly heavy ram had Holden stumbling backward. Eli was there to brace him. Still…

Sabra cried out. "Let me down."

Nova froze in an instant. "Too hard?"

"No. Not enough." She surprised him when she shoved his shoulders. He sat awkwardly. Holden set her on top of the much bigger man so that her knees were on either side of his hips. She pressed him the rest of the way to the floor. Lost in passion, she fished for Nova's cock.

Holden was there, lifting the thick, honeyed shaft and aiming it toward her core.

She didn't waste a moment.

Sinking on him until he filled her completely, she planted her feet on the floor then began to demonstrate the abdominal strength she'd honed. She rode him like a porn star with a heart of gold. Or at least that was what she was going for. Holden seemed to approve. He might even have drooled a little at the sight of her working Nova's beautiful, thick cock while her hands were planted on his tattooed chest.

Kaige grunted when she slammed onto him, though it would be impossible to hurt him with her slight weight. She gave him the fucking he wanted. Hard, rough and primitive. His head rocked on the carpet, his dreads swaying with in time to his grunts. Surprisingly, with him, she found her need morphed into something complementary, something she'd never felt before.

Power flowed through her as she realized she could affect such a strong man like this. More than just him. All of the Hot Rods. When Sabra glanced up, she realized it wasn't only her and Nova shattering boundaries. Kaelyn was sandwiched between Eli and Alanso while Bryce doted on Mustang Sally.

Holy shit. They'd started a trend.

Kaige seemed to notice the developments at the same instant. His head swiveled, gaze riveted to his fiancée as Roman and Carver tag teamed her, licking her pussy and sucking lightly on her ripening breasts. When she surrendered to orgasm, so did Kaige.

He gripped Sabra's hips and clamped her to him so that he was locked deep inside while he erupted, searing her tissue with the proof of his desire. With so many distractions, the first peak caught Sabra off guard. She flew into climax, shattering around Kaige and extending his blasts of come.

Before she could wilt, Holden caught her, lifting her off of Kaige, whose cock slipped from her along with a trickle of his seed. He flopped onto the floor, arms outstretched, and ordered Roman, "Bring Nola to me."

The woman nestled into the crook of his arm, then asked softly, "Feel better now?"

"Loads." He growled, then squeezed Nola. "Thank you."

"I think you dumped loads in Sabra. Jesus." Eli ragged on Kaige when he took a break from feeding Kaelyn his cock. "I saw your balls pumping like they were trying to put out a fire."

"Felt that way." Nova smiled at Sabra. "Rematch anytime. You were awesome."

"Same goes." She winked at him, then spun to face Holden. She had to know what he thought. Had it been what he truly wanted or only a fun fantasy?

The blaze in his eyes made it clear. He'd enjoyed it nearly as much as she had.

His mouth crashed onto hers as he probed her opening, toying with the evidence of Kaige's possession, using it to slick her clit and glide around the swollen nub. "I need you."

"I need you too." She guided his head back to hers for another taste of him.

When they broke for air, Holden asked, "Will someone fuck me while I fuck her? It's been a while. You'll have to go slow."

Carver raised his hand in a flash. "You'll be able to take me easiest. Plus, I'm a hell of a lot more gentle than that guy."

He jacked his thumb toward Barracuda.

"Did I give you my permission to fuck him?" Roman fired off the question.

"Since when do I need it?" Meep defied Roman for the first time since Sabra had been hanging around. She didn't want to be the cause of any tension, indirectly even.

"Guys, never mind." Holden waved at them, but they ignored him. "I'm cool."

"Stay out of this," Roman snarled. "It's between him and me."

"*You'll* be staying out of *me*." Meep's chest puffed up. "I'm not your bitch. When I bend for you, it's *my* choice. Fuck off. Lately, you don't deserve me."

Ouch.

Sabra winced.

"That's not news to me, Carver. I never deserved you." Barracuda stormed toward the door, pausing only to grab a pair of jeans and a white T-shirt from the pile of clothes on the couch. "I've got shit to do. I'll be in the garage. Fuck whoever or whatever you want, Meep."

"I would have anyway," Carver spat.

The glass rattled as the door slammed.

"There's always got to be one party pooper, right?" Meep tried to salvage the mood. Instead of making light of it, Sabra reached out. She drew Carver to her and Holden, then hugged him tight, wishing she could mend his cracked heart.

Holden surprised her, thrilled her, when he reached over and tipped Carver's mouth toward his. He placed a gentle kiss on his garagemate's mouth. At least that was how it started. Comfort transformed into longing by the time tongues flashed out to duel.

"It's going to be okay, Carver." Sabra rubbed his back as Holden distracted him. "Let Roman blow off some steam. You guys can make up tonight."

Meep moaned into Holden's mouth.

The sight of her boyfriend kissing another man renewed Sabra's arousal. She wasn't sure when Holden had shed his clothes, but he now stood there, naked, pressed to Carver. Similar in build, the two lean, compact men made a perfect match.

Especially with her in the mix.

Sabra didn't ask for permission. She reached down and took one of their cocks in each of her hands. Stroking them in unison, she adored the heat and slickness they coated her palms with. Finally, Holden broke the kiss, his cheeks red and his eyes bright.

"If we don't move along, I'm going to come in her hand. All over you," he told Carver.

"Doesn't sound like a bad thing to me," Meep said.

"You don't want to fuck me anymore?" Holden swallowed, then glanced away.

"Hell yes, I do." Carver reminded them all that he might be littlest, but he was fierce. He shoved Holden to the floor, then covered him, grinding his cock against Holden's ass.

"Yo, Meep," Alanso called out, then tossed a bottle of lube in their direction.

Those less dazed by lust helped coach the main players and keep them from hurting each other, even by accident. Eli made a recommendation. "Why don't you let him get inside Sabra first? He hasn't had someone play with his ass in a while. She can distract him while you get him ready and open him up. He'll enjoy it more that way."

"Good idea." Carver bit Holden's shoulder, then rolled off his friend. He took Sabra's hand and guided her to the floor.

"Holden, look what I have for you," Meep teased as he presented Sabra to her boyfriend as if she were a treat rather than a staple of his sexual diet.

It didn't take more than a heartbeat for Swinger to mount her and drive his cock into her depths. They both moaned at the familiar fullness. "Oh, fuck. You're soaked. Kaige really did fill you up. No wonder he knocked Nola up, if he always comes like that."

Sabra shuddered, her thighs hugging Holden as he began to swivel his hips. His cock felt right inside her. Comfortable. What she was used to and tuned to adore. Her body reacted instantly.

They got a little carried away. Fucking for his friends' viewing pleasure until Holden stiffened. "That's cold, Meep. Warm that shit up!"

"Who's the prankster now, Swinger?" Carver laughed as he poured fresh lube into his hand, then glossed his cock. "Remember those short straws? You just drew one."

The rest of the Hot Rods burst out laughing. Sabra would have to ask him why later. When she cared about anything except the pleasure he gifted her with.

"You ready?" Meep asked lower, more seriously.

"Yeah." Holden stilled. He grunted when Carver poked the tip of his cock inside the tight ring of muscle guarding his ass, then pressed insistently until Swinger's body admitted him.

"Wimp," Bryce teased. "You should try taking my cock up that tight ass."

"Um, okay." Holden glanced up then at Sabra. "Once I'm back in practice."

She held him, rubbing every inch of his skin she could reach in an attempt to soothe him while Carver penetrated him.

"Does this bother you?" Holden's lids drooped as Carver worked his dick deeper into Swinger's tight ass.

"Can't you feel my pussy about to strangle your cock?" She squeezed him for good measure.

"Uh, shit, yeah. I can feel that." He dropped his forehead onto hers. "So good. Perfect."

"Feels that way to me too." Carver ran his hands up and down Holden's back, grabbing his ass cheeks and parting them so he could probe deeper before beginning to pump his hips.

Sabra needed to feel him moving too. She rocked her pelvis, getting some of the friction she needed, though not enough.

"You have to fuck too, Holden." Alanso was experienced in threesomes. "She'll need that to get off."

"But if I do—" He cut off on a cry. "—I'll come too fast. Can't help it. Wanted this for so long."

"Don't hold back for me." Sabra kissed him sweetly, in opposition to the naughty writhing of their bodies. "I want you to come. To experience as much ecstasy as you can. I bet you'll make Carver shoot in your ass too. Do you want that? For him to fill you up?"

Holden was reduced to guttural rumblings of assent as he began to hammer into her then back onto Carver.

"Don't worry, Swinger," Bryce promised. "We'll take care of your girl. She won't be left hanging."

As if to prove his point, Rebel picked up the pace, driving Sally to what looked like an epic orgasm.

Holden pounded her and Carver simultaneously. He relied on his garagemates to keep their word. After bringing Sally down from her high, Bryce left her to cuddle with Kaelyn and joined Carver and Holden. Eli and Alanso did the same.

All three of them knelt with still-hard cocks aimed at the people fucking before them.

"Everyone else has had a chance to come with her, Holden. We should claim her too." Eli offered logic at a time when physical pressure had overruled brainpower.

So Sabra took matters into her own hands.

She stared into Holden's eyes as another man fucked him and he fed her his resulting hard-on with savage grace. "I want you to come with him. Show him how much you need him."

"Need you too," Holden said brokenly.

"Let me see. Come in me," she ordered.

And he obeyed.

Holden roared, the tendons in his throat standing out as he released his pent-up desire. He rutted on her like a maniac for several seconds before going stock-still. Carver however continued to fuck, tapping Holden's ass with his pelvis even as he shouted his own completion.

"I'm coming," Meep announced. "Can't stop. So fucking tight."

Holden moaned and shook. He came harder than she'd ever seen him come before.

Sabra wasn't the least bit jealous. Her chest expanded knowing she could give this to him. Be everything he needed by accepting his friends and their unique bond, which now extended to her as well.

As if they could read her thoughts, the guys peeled Carver from Holden and Holden from her. The men collapsed to the side, spent. Holden reached for Sabra's hand, entwining their fingers.

"Take good care of her for me." Holden asked the Hot Rods to be there for her and Sabra knew it had to do with more than sweaty sex. She thought of his mother for a brief moment and knew he was protecting her.

He truly loved her.

She could see it in his eyes as they gazed on her with such devotion it melted her heart.

"We will," Eli swore. "Just like you would do for our mates."

Holden nodded.

Coordinating without words, as men who've enjoyed women together often, Eli took his position between her legs, Alanso knelt by her head and Bryce straddled her torso. She opened her mouth and took Al inside, savoring the subtly of his flavor, spicy and distinct from the other men she'd sampled so far.

Cobra gave her more to consider when he pushed inside her, introducing her to his cock. Long, though thinner than Kaige's, his erection glided through her wetness in fluid strokes that held a lot more finesse than the raw fucking Nova had given her. She relished all their brands of loving.

Bryce easily palmed her breasts and molded them around his shaft. The force of his heavily veined cock strumming her nipples added another layer of sensation to the riot already bombarding her.

By now they were riding the edge of rapture.

Their fucking was the culmination of their exchange.

A pact. A bond. A promise.

She belonged to them now. And they to her.

The thought alone nearly shoved her into another orgasm. This one would either tear her apart or make her fly. She thought she knew which.

Sabra looked to Holden. He kissed each of her fingers as he let his friends ravage her. Encouraged them to. He watched the ritual fucking as if he'd never seen anything more beautiful. She was willing to perform for him every day of their lives if that revved his motor. Whatever kinks he had, she seemed to share the complementary version.

"Come on, baby," Kaelyn called from the sidelines. "Paint her with your come. Show her she belongs here."

Sanctuary at Hot Rods had been life-saving for Kae. She would understand.

Sally cheered on her guys too.

Soon the three of them were sweating as they fed her sensations upon sensations. And she couldn't possibly deny them for long.

Holden pushed her over the edge with the thing that mattered most. "I love you, Sabra."

With that, she shattered. She screamed around Alanso and milked Eli's cock. Bryce iced her chest, making sure to aim a jet of his come over her heart. None of it was lost on her. As she drank Alanso's release, she knew they were each a part of her now. And would be forever.

The men drifted away to tend to their own women, making sure everyone had survived their experiment intact. They had. Better for it.

Holden crawled to her. He paused to kiss her sloppy mound, then the tip of one breast and finally her lips. He didn't shy away from the proof of any of the men who had possessed her. In fact, he seemed reverent. More so with each contact.

"I love you too, Holden." She nuzzled into his embrace when he settled beside her and knew there was no other place in the world she should be right then.

"To our newest Hot Rod," Eli proclaimed.

Everyone cheered.

***

Sabra had nearly dozed off in Holden's arms when an enormous crash shook the foundation of the Hot Rods garage. "What was—?"

She hadn't even finished her sleepy question when Meep flew over her. The fastest Hot Rod didn't hesitate long enough to get dressed. He fled the room, shouting, "Roman!"

Shit, Barracuda was down there alone.

"You don't think he would have tried to hoist that engine by himself, do you?" Bryce wondered. People rummaged for their clothes on the floor. Within seconds, the guys followed Carver to the garage.

"Sabster, you'd better go get Tom." Alanso tagged her as he bolted past.

Holden kissed her forehead, then joined the rest of the gang, rushing to help Roman. The women took a few moments longer, needing to uncover bras and shirts instead of a simple pair of shorts or sweats in the commotion.

Sabra knew it was bad when a primal roar reached her ears. She hadn't gotten halfway down the stairs when screams and cursing echoed off the building. Turns out, she didn't need to get Tom. He raced across the lawn before she made it halfway there.

Surprisingly, Ms. Brown trailed after him.

Afraid of what she would find, Sabra ducked into the garage. The guys huddled around Roman, who writhed on the floor. Blood had soaked half of his T-shirt. It took her a second to realize that the white poking through the mess was actually the tip of his humerus.

Oh God.

She put out a hand to steady herself and found Sally doing the same. They hugged each other as the guys stabilized Roman. Carver was already on the phone calling 9-1-1. They needed an ambulance, quickly.

"Fuck. Fuck. Fuck." Barracuda snarled and cursed. "No. Not going to the hospital."

"Sure, dude," Nova yelled right back. "We'll just let you walk around here like some jacked-up scarecrow until you bleed to death."

Speaking of, Nola had approached with a section of rubber tubing. She wrapped it around Roman's upper arm and handed the ends to the guys to tie off. They applied pressure, keeping Barracuda as still as possible.

He railed against them. His gaze latched onto Carver. "Don't let them take me. Don't let them—"

Struggling against the guys, he accidentally knocked Kaelyn in the face with his elbow. She plopped backward onto her ass, grabbing her cheekbone.

Horrified, Roman froze.

"It was an accident." Carver instantly slid by his side. "She's fine."

Barracuda's face was so pale it seemed gray.

Using his reluctance to hurt a woman, Sabra, Nola and Sally entered the fray. Roman calmed instantly to avoid flailing into them. Carver sat behind him and propped up his torso to keep the injury as far above his heart as possible.

They were effective, but when Ms. Brown joined the women, petting Roman's hair and murmuring in his ear, he seemed transformed. His anger seeped out of him as surely as his blood. Almost worse, pain took its place.

He howled.

Tom took the hand of his uninjured arm and held tight. "I won't let them run tests on you other than your arm. I promise, Roman. They're not going to see. There won't be endless questions. You're an adult, not a child.

We'll get you back to work in no time. Nothing else."

"That's right," Ms. Brown crooned. "I'll stay with you the whole time. So will Carver. You're not alone. No one here did this to you. There's nothing to be ashamed of."

Sabra raised her brows and looked to Holden.

Outside, he mouthed.

The rest of the gang had Roman under control. They went into the fresh air, free of the iron tang of the garage, to wait for the paramedics. Sirens rang faintly in the crisp night air.

"If they x-ray him, they'll see how many times his bones have been broken." Holden scrubbed his hands over his face.

Sabra enfolded him in a hug and refused to let go. He trembled in her hold.

"He was abused," she stated.

Her boyfriend nodded, and the rapid bob of his Adam's apple as he swallowed stabbed her in the heart. "So bad. Horrible things. No kid should ever have to go through that. He hates hospitals. Hates doctors. His mom never even went with him. She left him out front so she wouldn't get in trouble, then took off for the next place. He kept finding her for a while. Trying to save her. He couldn't. He shouldn't have tried. All it got him was more trips to the hospital for his trouble."

"Hey, it's okay." Sabra went to her tiptoes to kiss Holden. He seemed to sink into her offering. "He survived before and he will again. He's a tough son of a bitch. Ms. Brown is going to go with him. She won't leave him for a second. Carver either. Us too. Let me drive, though."

"Okay." He leaned on her this time. It surprised her that he agreed. And filled her with joy. They could be there for each other. Would be. He trusted her, no matter what damage *his* mother had done.

If he could overcome his history. So could Roman.

"I love you, Holden," she reminded him. "We're going to get through this together."

"I love you, too."

EPILOGUE

Two weeks later, the pilot aired on national television. By the first commercial break, Sabra had three offers she didn't plan to take, the foundation had been flooded with donations and volunteers and the Hot Rods voicemail box had been blown to smithereens. If this kept up they'd have to think about opening that second location they'd discussed for the far, far future.

Maybe a separate motorcycle shop too.

Carver couldn't help but smile when he got sight of the Sabster practically skipping toward the garage after she exited her vehicle. A hell of a lot different than her approach after the pitch session with her old station. He might have been jealous of Holden if Swinger hadn't so graciously included the guys in their relationship. Hell, he hadn't seen his friend so blissed before—genuinely happy instead of merely encouraging everyone else to forget their troubles through an endless series of pranks. Finally.

"Yo, Swinger. Your girl is home." He gave his friend time to untangle himself from the red leather he installed in their latest project.

Good thing too, because when she approached she picked up steam until she threw herself into his arms and wrapped her impressively limber legs around his waist.

Carver grinned as he watched them suck face.

"I take it that went well?" Holden rubbed their noses together as he absorbed the positive energy practically radiating from the Sabster.

"Yup." She giggled, causing Swinger to groan. The guy had a serious thing for her laughter.

"Hey, everybody, come here!" Carver rounded up the gang.

They huddled around the pair, who refused to separate long enough to share the news in any dignified fashion. He liked this team meeting better than the one he couldn't shake from his nightmares, where Roman had sat in a pool of his own blood, not far away. Thankfully, a minor surgery later, a couple pins and a cast for a long fucking time, and the guy would heal. After all, he had a lot of experience in mending broken bones.

Carver shook his head to clear the troubling thoughts.

"We're the next big thing, right?" Kaige joked.

Except it seemed like it was true.

"Hell yes," Sabra confirmed. "Not only did the initial ratings set records nationwide, but it set off a major network bidding war. My old station canned Grills for letting the program slip through his fingers. He's under investigation for a slew of sexual harassment charges. They offered me a ridiculous deal to come back there, but no way. I can stick it to those bastards by going with someone else. Someone bigger. Fuck them and all the shit they put me through. Denver and his station took a chance on me that night and I'm staying with him."

Eli and Alanso high-fived as if her victory were their own. Because good shit for a Hot Rod was bonus for them all. There was no denying Sabra had become one of them in her own right and twice as much because of her relationship with Swinger.

They may not have formalized things yet, but they all knew she wasn't going anywhere.

Hot Rods were loyal for life.

Sabra squirmed until Holden let her down slowly, as if considering celebrating right there on the brand-new backseat he'd finished upholstering an hour ago. When she peered around at them, they each granted her support through their nods, smiles and congratulations.

"I guess it's up to you guys, though. If you'll let me stay. Let me film the show. You know...for the next two years that they offered to contract." She nibbled her lip as if any of them could deny her. Or wanted to.

"Two seasons? Seriously?" Holden grabbed her again and twirled her around. "You're amazing."

"Actually, more like three seasons. Seventy-five episodes. They're going to run new content more than a single time a year. It's a record offer for a new show, with options for add-on seasons." She sniffled a little, threatening to throw the shop into chaos with feminine tears. None of them were immune to that.

"Holy shit, girl. Way to go." Mustang Sally cheered from her place between Eli and Alanso.

Nola looked like she might pass out from excitement. "Do you know what this will do for the shop? Damn, Sabster!"

They all laughed when Nola took up Sabra's unofficial-official nickname while rubbing her own belly. Carver thought of their bright future and how their family had grown.

He couldn't wait to be part of that. With Roman.

Where was the guy, anyway?

Meep looked around, sudden dread eating through the rapture that had suffused him moments ago. Last time he'd gone missing hadn't ended so well.

In the distance he heard the rest of the Hot Rods negotiating to keep Sabra in the garage. Convincing her to let her lease expire when it came up for renewal the next month. A big step, though one they were ready for.

"It means you won't be able to get rid of me anytime soon," she tentatively offered with a rare hesitation in her voice.

"Exactly," Holden reassured her. "Where do I sign?"

He whipped a pen from the pocket of his coveralls and snatched her briefcase up, rummaging for the papers, making Sabra laugh.

"Wait. One more thing." She stayed him with a soft hand on his wrist. "There's a lot of money involved in this deal. What do you think about paying me a fair salary, then splitting the rest between the garage and the shelter? I'd like to fund as many adoption grants as possible with the proceeds."

Kaelyn cut in this time. As the office manager, she had their finances in better order than ever before. "The advertising is enough to support the shop. Put all the extra toward helping the kids."

She looked around, silently asking for everyone's agreement. With a nod, Carver gave his, edging from worry toward pissed that Barracuda was missing such a pivotal moment in their history.

Ms. Brown and Tom strolled in about that time. They seemed on better terms this past week, though the hints of their fledgling romance had all but disappeared. Carver planned to ask his dad what was up with that. Soon. As soon as he kicked Roman's ass for whatever trouble he was getting himself into instead of being in the garage. Despite his broken arm, there were things he could do to help. Or keep Meep company.

"Do you hear that, Tom?" Bryce shouted to the guy. "Sabster scored big time. Three seasons of *Hot Rods* are coming to a TV near you."

"You're going to be a star, Mom," Nola added.

As if whatever had happened between them disappeared for a moment, Tom and Ms. Brown turned to each other and shared a warm embrace. He whispered something in her ear and kissed her cheek, which led to catcalls, whoops and shouts of encouragement from the gang.

Blushing, Ms. Brown broke away.

"Better yet," Kaige added, "we're going to make a lot of people happy. Sabra is setting up adoption grants. The program should be named after her, don't you think?"

"Would you mind if we named it after my parents instead?" she asked.

Tom jogged across the concrete floor and stole Sabra from Holden for just a moment. He practically crushed her in a bear hug at the news. "That's perfect. You're a special kid, Sabster."

"Not you too," she laughed as she dropped her forehead on Tom's chest.

He ruffled her hair, then held her out to Holden, who reclaimed her as if he might wither if he didn't touch her again. Constantly.

Carver knew that craving. He had it himself.

Except the guy he'd like to think of as his lifeline had apparently vanished.

While the rest of the gang celebrated, Meep went on a search-and-rescue mission. What he found wouldn't be pretty. He braced himself. It wouldn't be the first time he'd seen Barracuda wrecked. But he'd thought him long past those days.

Why now?

What was bugging him? It had to be more than a broken bone—or even some quality time in the hospital complete with flashbacks to a childhood of abuse—hurting the man to regress him to these bad habits. Carver tried to understand, but it was tough.

It hurt to think that his love for Roman wasn't enough to heal the man.

Once he turned the corner out of the garage, he jogged up the stairs to their apartment. After checking their room and the main living areas, he gave up and scouted the roof deck. No luck there either. His car had been in the lot, so he couldn't have gone far.

Carver stomped down the stairs, heading for the only other likely place.

Sure enough, when he burst into the gardens behind Tom's house, Barracuda perched on a stone bench, listing to one side. His arm must have been killing him to affect him so much.

As relieved as Meep was, annoyance flashed out in its place.

"What are you doing out here? Couldn't you hear the shouting? Sabra's back. They offered her a three-season deal." Carver talked as quickly as he was known for running in an attempt to pretend shit wasn't as bad as it seemed.

"So go celebrate with them. You know Swinger will want you to nail her while he watches." Roman shrugged, the black cast on his arm barely moving as he nursed the injury.

"Since when is that a problem?" There were so many things going haywire, Carver didn't know where to start.

"Since never. It's fine. Not a peep outta me 'bout it." The other guy refused to meet his stare. What was this? Jealousy? "Go fuck 'er. Have fun. Not like you need me anyway. Someone else would be glad to pound your ass, I'm sure."

Carver might have thrown a punch then, if he hadn't realized how much Roman slurred his words. Not out of anger, but something...chemical. He peered at Barracuda and noticed a cloudiness to his dilated eyes.

When Holden spotted an empty, broken bottle in the weeds a few feet away, he charged for the largest shard of it.

"What the fuck is this?" He held up the demolished absinthe. No doubt Roman had polished off the liquor before smashing the container. "You're drinking *and* taking pain medicine? Barracuda, that shit is strong. Both of them. Are you stupid?"

The thought of what might have happened, with Roman out here alone—trashed—made his heart race.

Barracuda didn't bother to respond. Hell, he might not have heard Carver's tirade. He zoned out, his gaze unfocused in the direction of the koi pond and the mesmerizing flashes of orange that zipped by from time to time.

An easy target in his altered state, Roman didn't know what was coming until it was too late. Carver lunged for the bench and forced his hand in Barracuda's pocket. The guy grunted, probably hoping for a better sort of screwing than he was about to receive.

Meep wrested the bottle, which had caused the bulge he'd noticed, from Roman's pants. Not hard considering the loopy stare the other guy sported. He zipped away when Barracuda tried to grab him. Both of them knew he could outrun his roommate even when he was sober, so neither of them continued with pointless efforts.

Roman groaned and put his face in his good hand.

Carver shook the amber bottle. He could tell it wasn't as full as it should be. Still, he peeked inside and did a quick count. "Jesus, Roman. I just filled this prescription for you yesterday. How can you only have eight pills left?"

"Would you believe they fell down the drain?" His monotone didn't lend the lie much oomph.

"Fuck no." He plopped onto the bench, terrified when Roman seemed like he might fall off the other side. His arm snuck around his roommate's waist instinctively. "This is bullshit, Barracuda. Whatever's going on, this isn't how to solve your problems."

"I thought I could count on you to be with me instead of against me, Meep." Roman didn't beg for anything. That was about as close as he'd ever gotten.

"I've always got your back. And that's why I won't stand by while you do this to yourself." Carver squashed the urge to wrap his arms fully around Roman and take the easy way out, offering him physical comfort against emotional pain.

Meep loosely held his roommate, the man he loved more than anyone else on Earth. He wondered where he would find the strength to see them through this. Again. And what about next time?

Could he keep picking Roman up when he crashed?

What about the cost to himself? He didn't know if he was strong enough to bear the disappointment each time Barracuda stumbled into this dark abyss. Some days it felt like the blackness sucked the life out of him too, though he tried to be the light for his friend—and lover—to follow home.

"Meep, I'm tired." Roman voiced Carver's thoughts. Not unusual, honestly.

Except this time there was something frightening in the lethargic admission.

"Gonna go to sleep now, okay?" Barracuda's head lolled onto Carver's shoulder. "Don't leave me until it's over. Promise."

"What?" Carver sat up straighter, but Roman went limp in his arms. How much had he drunk? Had he taken all the extra pills this morning? Was the situation worse than he'd imagined? Feared. Surely, Barracuda wouldn't have intentionally tried to harm himself, would he?

Meep shook Roman, not caring if he jostled the guy's broken arm a bit. The pain would help him come more alert.

It didn't, though.

His dead weight seemed heavier than the times they'd leaned on each other when they were making love. No, this was like the old days, when Roman would often drink until he blacked out. Guzzle alcohol along with drugs by the fistful to numb his pain.

Back then he'd had quite a tolerance.

Maybe he'd overestimated himself. Maybe…

Carver put his finger to Roman's neck. The pulse beneath his flesh was slow and weak. Nothing like the man it beat inside. Something was wrong.

Really fucking wrong.

"Guys!" He shouted for the Hot Rods as he levered Barracuda into his arms then over his shoulder, hoping he didn't do more damage. "Help!"

He put his fingers in his mouth and whistled as loud as he could. Roman flopped onto his side.

"Someone fucking help me! Help Roman!" Carver didn't care if he sounded like a pussy. He screamed as he ran, slower than usual with the heavy load he bore. If ever he needed speed it was now. Tripping, he bobbled Barracuda, then leaned forward, tearing up the grass as he sprinted. *Come on!*

Buster McHightops zoomed out of the garage, barking his fool head off, and nipped at Carver's heels as he headed for his Roadrunner. The ruckus got the mechanics' attention and they poured from the bays like wasps from a kicked nest.

"My keys. Someone throw me my keys." He opened the door and placed Roman on the seat as gently as he could without taking too long.

Bryce called to Buster and the dog backed off. Within seconds, he was back, the keys dangling from his mouth. The rest of the Hot Rods were catching up, headed for their own rides. Kaige got there first and ducked in with Carver.

"What the fuck?" Nova roared.

Carver didn't wait to explain. With Kaige tending Roman, Meep tore out of the lot, gravel kicking up in every direction. While he drove, he spotted the rest of the Hot Rods not far behind in his rearview mirror.

"Overdose?" Kaige asked.

Carver gripped the wheel tighter and nodded. "I think so."

Kaige cursed violently, then started texting with one hand while hugging Roman to him.

Carver prayed they made it to the hospital in time.

There was never a better time to be a Hot Rod. Especially a fast one.

Meep slammed the pedal to the metal.

Some hearts can be repaired. Others should just be totaled.

Carver always thought he could sense when Roman was on the verge of falling into his inner darkness. But this time, Carver misses those cues—and leads the police on a high-speed race to the ER, praying his Barracuda won't die on the way.

When Roman awakens from the haze of painkillers and alcohol, he already knows the question poised on Carver's lips. Was it an accident—or did he deliberately dance on the edge of death? How can he tell Meep that lust and laughter are no longer enough to help him cope with the rapid changes among the Hot Rods?

Part of him is happy for them. The other part is pissed. Because what he's always wanted is Carver all to himself. Much as he loves his brother mechanics, sharing isn't his strong suit.

Roman needs time—and distance—to get his head on straight. The only question is, when Roman comes home from rehab, will Carver still love the man he has become—or will their roads have diverged too far to cross each other again?

EXCERPT FROM BARRACUDA'S HEART, HOT RODS BOOK 6

Crimson and blue lights flashed maniacally in the rearview mirror of Carver Levon's gleaming orange Plymouth Road Runner, which was no stranger to Middletown's police force.

That would usually have him raining F-bombs around the custom interior of his sweet ride. His license couldn't withstand the weight of any more points. Hell, his insurance had threatened to drop him the last two times he'd gotten pulled over. Skyrocketing rates were the only thing keeping them doing business with him at this point.

Today, Carver didn't give a damn.

Nor did he slow a single mile an hour.

In fact, he gripped the wheel tighter and pressed the pedal to the floor as wailing sirens inadvertently ushered slow-moving vehicles out of the way so that he could race toward the emergency room. He'd heard people describe tunnel vision before. In this life-or-death moment, all his senses were affected. Although he registered his friend and fellow Hot Rods mechanic Kaige Davis shouting something from the far side of the bench seat they occupied, the message didn't penetrate his ultimate concentration.

He refused to accept that Super Nova might be informing him their reckless sprint was unnecessary. Impossible. Hang on, Barracuda. We're almost there. Don't you fucking leave me now.

Downshifting, Carver resisted the urge to put his hand on the limp man beside him. Then he gunned it around a corner at a speed easily three times the legal limit. Sparks shot from the undercarriage as they rocketed into the hospital parking lot before screeching to a stop that tested the high performance porcelain brakes he and Roman had installed last summer.

He kicked open his door, not even wincing when it bounced against the hinges, then hauled his unconscious roommate over his shoulder before bolting into the one place Roman would hate waking up in. The cast stabilizing the guy's arm from his recent accident slammed a morbid beat into Meep's spine as if he were trying to object to a return visit.

I'm sorry, Cuda. They're going to help you. I promise. They have to!

A nurse skittered around the desk. She didn't bother to shout at Carver to stop or lecture him about protocol. Instead, she ushered him through a bright white mess of beeping machines. The smell of disinfectant seared his flaring nostrils while people bustled around them in what seemed like barely restrained chaos.

"What're we dealing with?" the nurse asked.

"Overdose." He winced even as he wanted to shake his precious cargo for being so damn selfish. Stupid…and in unfathomable pain.

"What substance?" the woman asked without judgment. Plenty of time for that later.

"Painkillers—oxycontin—and alcohol." Carver groaned. "Lots of booze, I think."

"Set him here." She patted a gurney before spinning away for supplies from a nearby cabinet while shouting some kind of code that drew a team of medical personnel toward them like a swarm of agitated bees. "Go. Let us work."

Carver couldn't bring himself to forsake Roman's uninjured hand. No matter how hard he tried, unfurling his fingers seemed impossible when it might be the last time he got to touch his best friend and lover.

"Sir." The nurse repeated herself a few times, not unkindly, though stern. "We're going to need you to wait outside."

He shook his head vehemently.

"I'll be quiet. Stay out of the way. Just...don't make me abandon him," he begged.

"Trust me. This isn't going to be pretty." She reached out as if she would brush the tears from his cheek, but he stumbled backwards.

Jesus, they were so fucked up, the pair of them. It could just as easily have been him on that table—seizing, limbs flopping, white foam building on lips he knew so well. Except he wasn't a quitter and he'd never choose to leave Roman.

"Go," the nurse urged again, respecting his aversion to the touch of a stranger. "They're going to need information from you. Quickly. His name, patient records, stuff like that so we can be most effective."

When Meep could only stare in shock and horror, she said the one thing that could budge his leaden feet.

"I'm no help to your friend if I'm sitting here babysitting you."

Putting himself in reverse, Carver refused to whisper goodbye, not even when the swinging door he backed through cut off his line of sight.

His knees buckled and he would have crashed to the over-waxed linoleum if Kaige hadn't been right there to grab him. Plucking him from midair, the man wrapped his arm around Meep's waist and lent him every bit of the considerable strength in his bulging biceps.

"Hey now," Nova grunted beneath Meep's dead weight. "I've got you. Over here, come on."

Kaige led him to the desk where the nurse gathered the required data. Rote answers slipped from Carver, who was dazed, unable later to recall a single thing she'd asked him.

After she released him, Carver couldn't sit, despite the heaviness in his gut that made him feel like he'd swallowed a few dozen ball bearings. Restless, he wished he could run. Like he had in his younger days when things had gotten too hard to handle. This time he had to stick around. For Roman.

"You can let go now." He dusted Kaige's hand off when he caught the interested glances they were garnering from some of the other patients in the lobby.

"Sure about that?" Super Nova wasn't fooled. "I don't give a shit about anyone but you. And Cuda."

"I got this." He nodded, attempting to convince himself.

"I'll be right here." Kaige relinquished his grip with a sigh before raking his hand through his blond dreads. He didn't waste another second before slipping his phone from his pocket and texting fast enough to make a teenaged girl envious.

Carver's knees knocked together. He braced his hands on his thighs then drew up, coaching himself mentally to take deeper breaths before he passed out cold. He paced, unable to simply sit by while his fate was decided.

As he made another circuit past the automatic door, his friends barreled inside.

Eli London's wrinkled brow, his father Tom's matching frown and Bryce's white-knuckled grip on his girlfriend Kaelyn's hand were bad enough. But the puffy redness marring Mustang Sally's pretty eyes stabbed him in the heart.

She wasn't the kind of girl to cry easily. Certainly not in front of strangers. Her agony confirmed his instinctive fears and eroded the hope he kept trying to manufacture.

Numb and utterly wrecked inside, he wobbled.

As he'd sworn, Kaige was there.

Carver leaned on Super Nova—the hell with anyone who didn't approve of their bond.

Nova didn't hesitate. He wrapped one tattooed arm around Carver's waist and acted like he had slung it there casually while he supported nearly all of Meep's weight. Too bad the guy couldn't breathe for him too. It felt like a semi—or five—had parked on Carver's chest and the lack of oxygen making it to his brain had everything spinning a million miles an hour around him.

All he knew for sure was that before long, he was surrounded in the embrace of his best friends, his family. Eli, Sally, Alanso, Bryce, Kaige and Holden. The misfit mechanics from the garage and the women they'd brought into their gang positioned themselves beside him. With them there, he was able to stand on his own. Nola, Kaige's pregnant woman, kissed Carver's cheek before rushing into her fiancé's now open arms. Sabra, Kaelyn and Nola's mom, Ms. Brown, took a turn surrounding Meep with their warmth and concern.

Still, none of their hugs felt like the one he wanted most.

He didn't dare try to speak, sure his voice would crack.

If he lost it, he wouldn't be able to put himself together again.

"I'm going to go take care of the paperwork." Ms. Brown hurried over to the nurse who waved a clipboard with a zillion additional forms fluttering from it in their direction.

With as much love surrounding him as he could hope for, Carver settled in.

It was a long wait, one that seemed endless.

He was sure he'd be bald from tugging on his own hair, and his stomach had started to growl like it was trying to eat itself, while shitty coffee corroded his guts. The other members of their gang took turns cursing, crying or holding his hand through the interminable hours.

But it was worth every horrific instant when a haggard looking doctor finally made it out to them and gave them guarded reassurance.

Roman was going to make it. Physically, he'd survived.

How pissed would he be about that?

Pretty irate if the next words out of the doctor's mouth were any indication. "I would normally let you pop in for a minute, but..."

He stared straight at Carver, probably because he'd already begun to edge toward the patient rooms.

"I'm sorry. Mr. Daily doesn't want visitors at this time."

"Fuck that! I'm not some kind of guest. I'm his—" Well, shit. When it came right down to it, Carver supposed he wasn't officially much of anything to the guy fighting for his life. Or trying to surrender it, maybe.

"Again, I'm sorry. Truly." The doctor attempted to squeeze Carver's shoulder, but he shrugged away from the unfamiliar contact.

He would have torn through the ward like the Tasmanian Devil instead of the Road Runner he was nicknamed for if it weren't for the man who intervened. Tom. The head mechanic's dad—surrogate father to all the Hot Rods—crossed his arms and stood with his feet spread, blocking a hell of a lot of the swinging door with his impressive frame.

"You can't be his medicine, son. Not this time. Roman's right. He's got to do this on his own."

Before he could stop himself, Carver whipped his phone from his pocket. Patients weren't supposed to have cells, but Hot Rods made their own rules. Cuda would get the message, when he felt like it.

I'll be here, whenever you're ready.

As if watching himself on TV, Carver dropped his hands and stared at his friends. "Someone drive me home?"

Everyone volunteered at once.

Why couldn't Roman ask them for help? Or simply accept it.

ABOUT THE AUTHOR

Jayne Rylon is a *New York Times* and *USA Today* bestselling author. She received the 2011 RomanticTimes Reviewers' Choice Award for Best Indie Erotic Romance.

Her stories used to begin as daydreams in seemingly endless business meetings, but now she is a full-time author, who employs the skills she learned from her straight-laced corporate existence in the business of writing. She lives in Ohio with two cats and her husband, the infamous Mr. Rylon.

When she can escape her purple office, Jayne loves to travel the world, SCUBA dive, take pictures, avoid speeding tickets in her beloved Sky and—of course—read.